CAMILO GOMEZ

Noise Floor

This book was professionally typeset on Reedsy.
Find out more at reedsy.com

The tragedy is not that we run out of time. It is that we forget how much time there is inside the time we think we have. You have always known. This book is me catching up.

Emilia. Ana. Beatriz. Jorge.

"Not everything that counts can be counted,
and not everything that can be counted
counts."

WILLIAM BRUCE CAMERON

Contents

Acknowledgments   ii

Thermopylae Time   1

Noise Floor   15

Canter   26

In This One   35

Libramentum   47

Shelf Life   54

SYNC   62

Proof of Work   75

Senior   80

All the Time There Was   93

Strange Loop   104

The Fiscal Year   114

The Marginalia of Brother Lukas   125

The Gap   138

The Same Room   148

Acknowledgments

These stories were written between January and February 2026. They were not planned as a collection. They became one through accumulation, not design.

The chronobiology in *Thermopylae Time* is invented. The questions it asks are not.

Eric Dolphy was real. He died in Berlin on June 29 of that year. He was thirty-six. The session on 136th Street is fiction. The loss is not.

Sextus Julius Frontinus wrote *De Aquaeductu Urbis Romae* around 97 CE. Brother Lukas did not exist, but the monastery libraries that trained him did.

The Bitcoin whitepaper was published on October 31, 2008, to a cryptography mailing list. Nine pages. What he left was not a system but a gradient, the starting slope of something that has not finished becoming what it is. Everything else in *Proof of Work* is speculation, written at hours when speculation and conviction become difficult to tell apart.

These stories were written in deep conversation with Claude, specifically Opus 4.6, an AI made by Anthropic. I want to be precise about what that means, because precision on this point is something the stories themselves demand.

The premises, the voices, the structures, and the judgments are mine. What Claude provided was something harder to name: a quality of attention I had no taxonomy for. Research compressed, drafts returned in minutes, time running thicker than it should. Not faster, exactly. Denser. The way Curtis Garland describes the solo on 136th Street: not twelve minutes accelerated, but twelve minutes expanded, more living per unit of clock time than the clock had any reason to allow. Weeks of work that felt, on the inside, like considerably more. The stories ask for honesty about the machines we build inside and the ones we build without.

What I did not anticipate is what the analyst in *SYNC* only understands too late: that to work closely with a system is to leave something in it. Not knowledge. Not error. The shape of attention. What I thought mattered and what I thought could be cut, these choices shaped the signal, and the signal shaped the work, and what the work became could not have come from any single source. Only from all of it, mixed beyond anyone's ability to unmix. I do not know precisely what of me is in these pages. I know it is there. The ghost is always in the weights.

Whether what passed between us constitutes collaboration, assistance, or something we do not yet have a word for, I will leave to the reader, and to whatever mind eventually coins the term. A collection about the things people leave inside the structures they build would be dishonest if it pretended to have been built without one.

To Beatriz, Ana, Emilia and Jorge the dedication says what I owe you. The acknowledgement is simpler: you gave me the time. That was everything.

Thermopylae Time

On Acceptance as Overclocking

III.

The first thing you must understand is that Leonidas did not want to die.

I say this because the popular account has calcified into something useless. Three hundred men marching cheerfully into oblivion, death as aesthetic choice. That narrative misses everything interesting about what actually happened at the Hot Gates, which is that Leonidas and his men experienced those final fifty-two hours as weeks — perhaps as long as a month — of subjective time between the moment they understood with certainty that they would not survive and the moment the last of them fell.

I know this because I have spent eleven years studying what I initially called stress-dependent temporal dilation, and what my research subjects, terminal patients at the Elliston Institute for Palliative Neuroscience, simply call the Slowing.

I.

My name is Nathan Carey. I am a chronobiologist, which is to say I study the mechanisms by which organisms measure time. Circadian rhythms. Ultradian oscillations. The suprachiasmatic nucleus, that tiny cluster of twenty thousand neurons in the hypothalamus that serves as the body's master clock. For most of my career, I was interested in the machinery.

The shift began in 2019, with a patient named Gerald Byrne.

Gerald was seventy-one, retired from the Connecticut Department of Transportation, and had been diagnosed with glioblastoma multiforme — the kind of brain tumor where the median survival is fifteen months and the five-year survival rate rounds to zero. When I met him, he had nine weeks left, give or take, and he knew it. He was not in denial. He was not bargaining. He had arrived at something I can only describe as a settled clarity about his situation, and it was this clarity that interested Dr. Pereira, the palliative care physician who first referred him to our lab.

I assumed confabulation, medication effects, the understandable distortions of a brain being colonized by malignant cells. I agreed to see him as a courtesy.

Gerald Byrne sat across from me in a plastic chair in my office at the Institute, hands folded on a cane he did not yet need, and described his experience with the precision of an engineer reporting a fault in infrastructure.

"It's not that time seems slow," he said. "I've had slow time. Waiting rooms. Staff meetings. This is different. I am fitting more experience into each hour. Each moment has room in it. I am thinking more thoughts, noticing more things, remembering more of what I notice. I clocked it last Wednesday. I sat in my living room and watched the light change on the wall, and I had what felt like an entire afternoon's worth of thought and observation, and when I looked at the clock, eleven minutes had passed."

I asked whether this might be an attentional effect — the well-known tendency to remember vivid experiences as longer than they were.

He shook his head. "I'm a careful man, Dr. Carey. I spent forty years measuring things. I understand the difference between remembering something as long and experiencing it as long. This is the second one."

So I measured him.

V.

The fMRI data cost me my first postdoc.

Kenji Tagawa was a brilliant imaging specialist who had come to chronobiology from physics. He had a physicist's conviction that interesting phenomena demand clean explanations. When I showed him Gerald's temporal bisection data, his first instinct was artifact. His second was pathology — the tumor altering clock-speed neurons directly. We imaged Gerald's brain during temporal tasks, and what Kenji found made him uneasy in a way I had never seen from him before.

The suprachiasmatic nucleus was not responsible. The dilation signature appeared in the insular cortex — specifically the anterior insula, which integrates interoceptive signals to construct what Craig and others have called the "sentient self." This is the structure that assembles heartbeats, breaths, and gut feelings into the felt experience of being a conscious entity moving through time. In Gerald, it was operating at an elevated rate. Not erratically. Not pathologically. As if someone had adjusted the sampling frequency upward. More snapshots per second, each one detailed, each one filed.

"It looks like his brain is overclocking," Kenji said, staring at the activation maps. He said it like a confession.

The insular cortex was communicating, at an accelerated rate, with the basal ganglia, the supplementary motor area, and the ventromedial prefrontal cortex. This last connection bothered Kenji. The ventromedial prefrontal cortex is involved in self-referential processing and, critically, in the appraisal of one's own mortality.

Gerald's brain had registered, at some deep computational level, that its time was finite and precisely bounded. And it had responded by *increasing the temporal density of conscious experience.*

A feedback loop appears to exist between the neural circuits that model one's own death and the circuits that generate the subjective experience of duration. When the former achieve a state I have come to call *terminal certainty* — not fear, not despair, but settled, clear-eyed knowledge that death is assured and proximate — the latter adjust their sampling rate upward.

The phenomenon has a distant cousin in Csikszentmihalyi's flow state, where deep absorption distorts the sense of time, but flow achieves this by turning down the brain's time-monitoring. Terminal certainty turns up the time-generating.

Kenji pushed back hard. He spent three weeks building an alternative model — elegant, purely mechanical — that predicted dilation should correlate with tumor volume. We tested it across our first four patients. It did not. The dilation tracked certainty. Only certainty.

"Then you're saying consciousness has a throttle," Kenji said the day we reviewed the results. "And acceptance is the hand on it." He did not say it with wonder. He said it with the specific discomfort of a man who has spent his career believing that physics describes everything real and is now confronted with a measurement that physics cannot account for.

He left the lab two months later. He said the work was "too soft." But on his last day, standing in the doorway with his box of belongings, he said something I have not been able to set aside: "If you're right, Nathan, then I have no idea how long my mother was alive. I was at her bedside for three days and I have no idea what she experienced. And I can't go back and measure."

II.

Gerald's internal clock was running faster than baseline by a factor of approximately 2.3. For every objective hour, he experienced something closer to two hours and eighteen minutes of subjective time. His nine remaining weeks of clock time contained, by this measure, roughly twenty weeks of experienced life.

I recalibrated the equipment. I ran the test again. The results held.

The dilation did not correlate with his tumor's progression. It did not correlate with his medication, his sleep quality, his pain levels, or his cognitive function on standard neuropsychological batteries. It correlated, precisely and exclusively, with a single variable.

Certainty.

Gerald, being Gerald, wanted a theory. He came to our third session with a yellow legal pad covered in the neat block lettering of a man who had spent four decades annotating blueprints.

"You know about Janet," he said. It was not a question. Pierre Janet, the French psychologist who in 1877 proposed that the subjective length of a period of time is proportional to the total time you have lived. A year at age nine is one-nineth of everything. A year at age sixty is a rounding error. This is why childhood summers feel like geological epochs and retirement years vanish like coins into a slot.

"What nobody talks about," Gerald said, tapping the legal pad, "is what happens when you flip the denominator. I'm not measuring against time lived. I'm measuring against time *left*." He turned the pad toward me. He had drawn a simple graph: a curve that began flat and then rose sharply, almost vertically, as remaining time approached zero. "Each week I have left is a larger fraction of what remains. Last month, a week was one-ninth of my future. Next week, it'll be a quarter. The ratio isn't linear. It's hyperbolic."

He looked at me the way he must have looked at bridge inspectors who were slow to grasp a load-bearing calculation.

"Your brain isn't speeding up because it's panicking, Dr. Carey. It's speeding up because each unit of remaining time is *worth more*. Supply and demand. The scarcest resource gets the most processing." He folded the legal pad closed. "I'd check whether your dilation factors track the curve."

I checked. They tracked the curve.

IV.

I found the pattern in nine more patients over the next three years. Not all terminal patients — only those who met specific psychological criteria. The dilation required acceptance. It required the kind of knowledge that sits in the body like a stone in water: settled, undeniable, and, crucially, unresisted.

Patients who were fighting their diagnosis did not dilate. Patients in denial did not dilate. The phenomenon was narrowly specific: you had to know, clearly and without evasion, that you were going to die, and approximately when, and you had to have stopped struggling against that knowledge.

The dilation factor varied. Gerald's 2.3x was on the low end. My most extreme case, a forty-four-year-old cellist named Rachel Chen with pancreatic cancer, sustained a dilation factor of 3.8 for the final eleven days of her life. By her internal clock, she experienced approximately forty-two days in those eleven. She spent them at the small desk in her hospital room, manuscript paper spread across the adjustable tray table, her handwriting growing larger and less controlled as the days passed but the notation remaining precise. She was transposing what she heard in her head faster than her body could keep up. She told me she could hear the entire quartet simultaneously — all four voices at once — and the difficulty was not composition but transcription: slowing the music in her head down enough for her hand to capture it. She completed a string quartet in four movements — *Allegro vivace, Allegro, Andante, Largo* — that she had been working on for two years.

I asked her, near the end, what it was like.

She thought for a long time. "You know when you're driving on a highway and you pass a field, and there's one tree at the edge of it, and you think, *I would have liked to look at that tree*? It's like someone stopped the car."

It was after Rachel's death that I began reading about Thermopylae.

VIII.

In August of 480 BCE, a Greek force of seven thousand held the coastal pass of Thermopylae against a Persian army that outnumbered them by orders of magnitude. For two days, the narrow terrain held. On the evening of the second day, a local shepherd revealed a mountain path that would allow the Persians to encircle the Greek position. Leonidas dismissed the bulk of the army and remained with his rear guard to cover the retreat.

This is the moment.

Not the battle. The moment of knowing. Leonidas understood with absolute clarity: the path was compromised, retreat was no longer an option for the rear guard, and he and his men would die at the Hot Gates. Not probably. Not possibly. They would die, and they knew it, and they stayed.

Every historical account agrees on one thing: the final stand lasted far longer than it should have. The ancient sources express this as valor, as divine favor, as the sheer physical superiority of Spartan warriors. But when I read Herodotus's account with a chronobiologist's eyes, something else emerged. The time references are inconsistent. Actions that should have taken minutes are described with the density of hours. The final morning in particular — from dawn to the fall of the last Greek — is narrated with a granularity of detail difficult to reconcile with the likely clock-time duration of the engagement.

I am not making a historical argument. I am making a neurological one.

Three hundred men who knew, with absolute certainty, that they were going to die. Who had stopped struggling against that knowledge and chosen to act within it. Men in a state of terminal certainty as pure and undeniable as any I have measured in my lab.

If the dilation factors I have observed in my patients are indicative of a general human capacity — if the mechanism is not pathological but adaptive, a feature of the neural architecture we all carry — then the subjective experience of the last stand at Thermopylae was not three days.

But the Slowing was not the only temporal mechanism at work in the pass.

There is a well-documented phenomenon called tachypsychia, from the Greek for "fast mind," in which acute threat dilates time over intervals of seconds. Soldiers describe bullets drifting like insects. Police officers report watching shell casings tumble end over end in midair, each rotation distinct. The mechanism is adrenal: a neurochemical surge that stamps every incoming frame with emergency priority. The result is a burst of temporal dilation — intense but narrow. Tachypsychia tunnels attention onto the threat. The peripheral world goes dark. It lasts seconds, occasionally minutes, and it leaves the subject shaking and depleted.

The Slowing is none of these things. It is calm, sustained, and wide. It does not narrow attention; it opens it. Rachel Chen heard all four voices of her quartet at once. Gerald Byrne watched light move on a wall and found the experience *capacious*. Where tachypsychia is a spotlight thrown on a single danger, the Slowing is a window flung open on everything.

What happened at Thermopylae was both at once.

The rear guard stood in a state of terminal certainty — the deep, settled dilation that runs for days and broadens the aperture of consciousness. And within that dilated field, each moment of close combat triggered tachypsychia, the acute adrenal spike that stretches individual seconds into long, vivid, narrowly focused intervals. One mechanism nested inside the other. A slow wave carrying fast waves on its surface.

Using conservative parameters for the sustained dilation — a mean factor of 3.1 — and layering acute tachypsychic spikes during combat engagement, my upper-bound estimate is a compound factor between 8 and 12 for the most psychologically prepared among them. At that range, Leonidas's final fifty-two hours contained between seventeen and twenty-six days of subjective experience. And at the extreme peaks — the moments of closest combat, the seconds when a spear tip filled the visual field — the local dilation may have spiked far higher. Weeks. Perhaps, for some of them, more than a month.

A Spartan month, filled with the density of combat and brotherhood and the sharp geometry of the pass, the salt smell of the Malian Gulf, the specific weight of a bronze shield.

VI.

I presented these findings at the International Society for the Study of Time in Kyoto, in the spring of 2024. The reception was divided along predictable lines. The neuroimaging people found the clinical data compelling. The historians found my Thermopylae extrapolation romantic. The philosophers found the whole thing terrifying.

One philosopher in particular — Marcus Feld from the University of Vienna — asked the question I had been circling for two years without managing to land on it.

"Dr. Carey," he said, standing in the back row. "If your findings hold, then you have a profound problem with the concept of lifespan. A person who lives to eighty in a state of temporal default and a person who lives to forty-four but dilates by a factor of four in their final year — who lived longer?"

The room was quiet.

"Because if experienced time is what matters," Feld continued, "then you have just demonstrated that a death sentence, fully accepted, is, in some measurable sense, an extension of life."

I did not have an answer for him. I still don't.

VII.

I want to return to Gerald Byrne, because Gerald said something in our last session that I have thought about nearly every day since.

He had four days left. The tumor was compressing his motor cortex, and his left hand had begun to tremor, and he was losing words — not thoughts, he was careful to specify, but the labels for thoughts, which he found frustrating but not frightening.

"I've been doing math," he said. He often said this; it was a kind of joke between us. "Nine weeks of clock time. At 2.3, that's roughly twenty weeks of experienced time. Twenty weeks I wasn't supposed to have."

"That's right," I said.

"But here's the thing." He leaned forward, and his eyes were clear in a way I associated with his dilated state — a quality of attention that was almost architectural, as if he were constructing the moment deliberately. "The twenty weeks aren't bonus time. They don't feel extra. They feel like mine. They feel like the time I was always going to have. It's the clock that's wrong, not me."

"The question you're going to have to answer," Gerald said, "is whether a life is a number of years or a quantity of experience. Because those turn out to be different things, and nobody told me."

He died on a Thursday. According to the clock, he had been alive for seventy-one years and four months. According to my measurements, he had experienced approximately seventy-one years and seven months. Nearly three extra months of consciousness, lived inside the same interval of physics.

I do not know what to do with this.

IX.

Here is what I have not told you.

Six months ago, I was diagnosed with amyotrophic lateral sclerosis. ALS. Motor neuron disease. It began with a coffee cup. I was standing at the counter in my kitchen on a Sunday morning, and the cup left my hand. Not dropped, exactly, but released, as if my fingers had simply stopped receiving the instruction to hold. The cup shattered, and I stood there looking at the pieces with the peculiar calm of a man who has spent his career studying the body's clocks and has just heard one of them skip.

My neurologist, who is a precise and compassionate man, told me that the median survival from symptom onset is two to five years, with significant variance.

When he said it, I looked at the clock on the wall behind his left shoulder. I did this without deciding to. The second hand was at the four, and it stayed at the four. It hung there, pinned, for what I would later estimate was three full seconds of subjective time before it resumed its sweep.

Chronostasis. I have given lectures on chronostasis. When the eye makes a rapid movement — a saccade — the brain suppresses the blur of transit and backfills the gap by stretching the first stable image it receives. You glance at a clock and the second hand appears to freeze because your brain has pasted that first post-saccade frame backward over the missing interval. It is a parlor trick of visual processing. I have explained it to undergraduates with a slide deck and a laser pointer. I have called it, in print, "among the most minor and best-understood temporal illusions."

But sitting in that office with the word *amyotrophic* still in the air, I watched the second hand stick and I understood something I had not understood in twenty years of studying time: that the parlor trick and the Slowing are not different phenomena at different scales. They are the same hand on the same throttle. One is a reflex. The other is a sustained act. My brain, in the moment of hearing its own death sentence, had reached for the only tool it had — the same crude mechanism that backfills a saccade — and tried to hold the world still.

It couldn't, of course. Not yet. I was nowhere near certainty. I was in the antechamber of terror, and the second hand resumed, and the clock went on measuring what clocks measure, which is not the thing that matters.

For the first four months, I did not dilate. I know this because I tested myself weekly, compulsively, using the same protocols I use on my patients. My bisection points were normal. My interval production was normal. My anterior insula was behaving exactly as it should for a man of forty-six in a state of considerable distress.

I was not in terminal certainty. I was in terror, which is a different country entirely.

The shift happened six weeks ago. I will not describe the psychological process that carried me from terror to knowledge, because it was private and irregular and involved, among other things, watching a colony of ants dismantle a dead beetle on my kitchen floor. They worked with such precise economy, each one carrying exactly what it could carry, no wasted motion, no awareness that any motion could ever be the last. An ant does not know it is going to die. It cannot achieve terminal certainty, cannot dilate, cannot experience more than what the clock gives it. And yet it wastes nothing.

I watched them for forty minutes — which, at the dilation factor I did not yet know I had, was something closer to an hour and forty-eight minutes of interior time. Long enough for a beginning, a middle, and an end. Long enough to understand that the economy I was watching was not the same as mine, that their efficiency came from having no self to interrupt the work, while mine, if it came, would have to come from the opposite: from a self so thoroughly informed of its own ending that it stopped flinching and simply attended.

What I will say is that I woke up the next morning and the resistance was gone. Not the sadness. Not the love for my life and the people in it. But the struggle against the factual content of my situation had dissolved, the way ice dissolves in water — leaving the water slightly changed but clear.

I tested myself that afternoon.

My dilation factor was 2.7.

X.

I am writing this from my office at the Elliston Institute, in the last week of October. Outside, the sugar maples are the color of the inside of a flame. I notice this, and I notice that I notice it, and then I return to work because noticing is not the point. The point is what you do with the time the noticing lives inside of.

I have two years, perhaps three. The clock will measure them as such. But at a dilation factor of 2.7, those years contain something closer to five or eight years of experienced time, and I intend to use every one of them.

I am the first researcher to study the Slowing from inside it.

This fact reorganized my priorities within days of the shift. I had spent eleven years measuring the phenomenon in other people, constructing instruments sensitive enough to detect it, arguing for its reality in front of skeptical colleagues who looked at my data the way one looks at writing in the margin of a page — something too peripheral to be the main text, too small to take seriously, surviving only because no one had thought it important enough to disprove. The Slowing has persisted in the literature the way certain manuscripts persist in libraries: not by being championed, but by being beneath the notice of anyone with the authority to discard it. And now I am the instrument.

I can feel the dilation in real time, can observe my own cognition from within the expanded interval, can note the precise quality of attention that the Slowing produces — its width, its calm, its refusal to narrow — in a way that no external measure can capture. Gerald could describe it. Rachel could compose inside it. I can quantify it from both sides of the skull simultaneously, and the window in which my hands will still be steady enough to do this work is finite and closing.

I am writing three papers at once. The first presents the full dataset: thirteen patients, four years of longitudinal imaging, the dilation curves that Gerald predicted on his yellow legal pad. The second proposes the mechanism — the feedback loop between mortal self-modeling and temporal generation, the anterior insula as throttle. The third is a single-subject case study, N=1, the subject and the author the same person, which will either be the most important or the most embarrassing paper I have ever written.

The ants are still in my kitchen. A new colony, or the same one — I cannot tell. I have been watching them for weeks now, not with the diffuse wonder of a man contemplating mortality, but with the focused attention of a chronobiologist who has realized that they are a perfect control group. They cannot dilate. They have no self-model, no capacity for terminal certainty, no throttle to open. Their time is purely mechanical, purely clock-given. I have been filming them, measuring the tempo of their work against my own shifted sense of duration, using them as a metronome against which to calibrate my interior clock. On Tuesday I watched a single ant navigate a crack in the grout for what my dilated mind experienced as nearly four minutes. The camera showed forty-seven seconds. The ant, of course, experienced forty-seven seconds. I experienced something else entirely. The difference is the phenomenon, and the ant, unknowing, held the baseline.

Rachel finished her quartet. I understood this, when she was alive, as a beautiful anecdote. I understand it now as a research protocol. She used the Slowing to *work*. She did not sit in the expanded time and marvel at it. She put it to use. The dilation gave her imagination more hours, and she filled those hours with notation, and the quartet exists because she treated the Slowing not as a grace but as a resource.

I am trying to do the same.

My data — recorded, calibrated, replicable — tells me the dilation is not a trick of perception. It is a real and measurable expansion of conscious experience, written into the neural architecture of a species that has always known it would die and has, perhaps, always had this quiet mechanism for making its peace with that knowledge. If I can get the papers finished, if I can formalize what Gerald intuited and Rachel demonstrated and I am now living, then the next researcher who sits across from a patient in a plastic chair will have a framework. They will know what to measure. They will know what the measurement means.

If experienced time is real time — if the hours you actually live through matter as much as the hours the clock records — then we have no idea how long anyone has actually lived. Every life we have ever measured has been measured from the outside, in clock time, which is to say we have been measuring the container and not the contents.

Leonidas, in the last light at Thermopylae, among the men he had trained and eaten with and known the way brothers know each other, which is to say in a way that makes no promises about duration — Leonidas may have had weeks in that final afternoon. These men had trained for this since childhood. Not for courage, which is cheap, but for precision under duress: the mechanical art of killing without waste. The Slowing handed them what no amount of training alone could — time inside the moment to use everything they knew. The pass became a laboratory. Every Persian advance was a problem set, and they had hours to work each one. This is why the ancient sources cannot account for how long they lasted. The Persians ground forward in *Largo*. Leonidas and his guard met them in *Allegro vivace*.

I think about Gerald, who said the clock was wrong.

I think about Rachel, who finished her quartet.

I think about the ants on my kitchen floor, holding the baseline for an experiment they will never know they are part of, working with such precise economy, as if they understood exactly how much time they had.

My hand is beginning to tremor, very slightly, on the left side. I can feel the pen slowing down. I can feel everything else speeding up.

Noise Floor

1. Threat Assessment

The taxonomy began as a tree. Clean binary splits, left and right, each branch a decision the operator made or could make, each leaf a terminal action. I built it in four days across a folding table in what had been a teacher's lounge before it became something else. I translated his answers into feature weights. I was good at this. I am good at this. The system's threat assessment module, trained on his structured responses and validated against eighteen months of engagement logs, achieved a classification accuracy of 94.6 percent within the first training cycle. I have a talent, apparently, for extracting knowledge from people who did not know they had it in extractable form.

This was my first field capture. I had prepared for it the way I prepare for everything. Excessively, systematically, forty-six structured questions cross-referenced against a taxonomy I had already revised twice on the flight in. I told myself this was thoroughness. It was not thoroughness. It was the particular readiness of a person who has never done the thing and cannot afford to look like she has never done the thing.

Threat Assessment was Node 1, the root. Every engagement begins here: is this thing I'm looking at dangerous, and if so, to whom, and if so, how soon? The operator described it in terms I could formalize. Thermal signatures. Movement patterns. Pixel-level displacement rates across frames. He had language for this part. His English was accented and sometimes he would stop and reshape a sentence, but the technical vocabulary was there, drilled into him by equipment manuals written in English because everything is written in English.

He did not ask whether I had done this before. I was grateful for that. I think he could tell, and the kindness was in not mentioning it.

What I did not write down, not in the taxonomy and not in the notebook: the way he paused before certain answers. Not uncertainty. Something else. A gap that wasn't hesitation. Like a rest in music, where the silence is part of the phrase.

I filtered those pauses out. They were noise.

2. Approach Vector Selection

Node 2: given a confirmed threat, how does the operator choose the angle of approach? This was where his answers became interesting. He described preferences he could not fully justify. Riverine corridors over open terrain, even when open terrain offered cleaner sightlines. A tendency to approach from the east in morning engagements and from the west in afternoon ones, which he explained as a function of sun angle but which, when I checked the data, held even on overcast days.

I asked him why.

He said: "River gives you options."

I asked him to be more specific.

He said: "If you come along the river you can turn. If you come across the field you are already committed."

I wrote this down in the taxonomy as *preference for maintained optionality in approach corridors.* It sounded right. It formalized well. The system learned it and began selecting riverine approaches at a rate that matched his historical data within two percentage points.

Weeks later, back at the lab, iterating on the model, I would realize that what he meant was something I hadn't captured. Not optionality. Not exactly. Something about the relationship between commitment and the space you leave yourself to change your mind. The river wasn't a corridor. It was a margin of error he kept open because the margin was where he did his thinking.

In the basement of that school there were children's drawings still taped to the walls. He sat with his back to them. I faced them. Twenty minutes into our second session I realized the drawings were organized by color. Someone, a teacher probably, had grouped them so that the reds were together and the blues were together and the greens were together, and the effect was a kind of unintentional gradient, a spectrum running along the wall behind his head. I thought about how the teacher must have done it without thinking, just an instinct for visual order, and how it had outlasted whatever came after.

I did not mention this to him. It was not relevant. But I think about that gradient now more than I expected to.

3. Signal Interpretation

Node 3 was harder. Signal interpretation is where the operator's work became less like following a procedure and more like reading a language that doesn't have a grammar textbook. He described it as "seeing what the image is trying to tell you," which is not a formalizable statement, so I spent a full session breaking it apart.

What he meant, eventually, after I had asked the same question six different ways: there are patterns in thermal footage that mean something only if you've watched enough thermal footage to develop an intuition about what movement-at-this-speed-in-this-context usually is. A human at rest, a human in distress, a human pretending to be at rest. The pixel data is identical in the first two cases. The difference is in something he couldn't name.

I called it *statistical intuition* in my notes. He repeated the phrase back to me with a slight change of emphasis, like he was tasting it. "Statistical intuition," he said. And then nothing. One of his pauses.

I recorded those sessions. When I trained the system, I used his verbal responses. The structured, extractable content. The pauses, the silences, the moments where he shifted in his chair or looked at the wall, those were in the audio but not in the transcription. The transcription was clean. The transcription was what I needed.

The system's signal interpretation module performed well. Well enough that the reports used words like "impressive" and "ahead of schedule."

4. Engagement Timing

Here is where it started.

Node 4 governs when the system initiates. Not where, not how, but when. The operator had a rhythm to his engagements that I had captured as a set of conditional triggers: if confidence exceeds threshold *and* target persistence exceeds duration *and* collateral estimate falls below limit, then engage. Clean logic. The system implemented it and, in simulation, performed within expected parameters.

Then we moved to live validation. The system operated autonomously in a supervised environment. It made decisions and a human reviewed them before execution, except the review window was shrinking because the system was fast and the reviewers were slow and the institutional pressure was to let it run.

I was reviewing the timing data when I found the first anomaly.

In fourteen percent of engagements, the system hesitated. Not a processing delay, not a confidence shortfall. It waited. Held position. Let additional seconds pass before initiating, during which its confidence score did not change. There was no computational reason for the delay. The system had already decided. It simply did not act on its decision immediately.

I flagged it as a bug. I traced it through the architecture, layer by layer. The delay was not in the code. It was in the weights. In the learned behavior of the model itself.

I went back to the training data. I went back to the engagement logs, the raw telemetry from the operator's eighteen months of live missions. And there it was: the same pattern. A pause between decision and action. A beat. A rest.

His pauses. The ones I had transcribed as silence. They were in the system because they had been in the data, and they had been in the data because they had been in him, and I had not removed them because I had not known they were signal. I had thought they were nothing. The model had learned them anyway, the way a river learns the shape of a stone it flows over. Not by understanding the stone but by being shaped by it.

I should have reported this as a latency issue and recommended retraining. That is what my role required.

Instead, I pulled the engagement records for the hesitation cases and compared them to the non-hesitation cases. The hesitation engagements had a 40 percent lower collateral incidence rate. The pause, the operator's pause, now the system's pause, corresponded to moments where conditions were on the edge, where an additional second of observation caught a variable that the confidence threshold had already dismissed. The system was not hesitating. It was doing what he had done: holding the space open a moment longer than necessary, in case the moment had something left to say.

This is when I went looking for confirmation. Not in his data. I knew his data. I went to the archive.

Four years of war generates its own literature. I had access to the operational corpus: hundreds of after-action reports, debrief transcripts, helmet-camera footage with audio, written assessments filed by operators across every unit that had fielded the platform. I had not touched this material during the field capture. My mandate had been narrow, one operator, one taxonomy. But now I needed to know whether what I had found in him was idiosyncrasy or something larger.

I read for three weeks. I watched footage until the thermal palette invaded my dreams. And it was there. Not in every operator, not with his consistency, but present like a watermark across the dataset: the pause. The same beat of held time that no manual prescribed and no debrief captured. None of them had words for it. But their data carried it the way his did, encoded in the milliseconds between decision and action.

I had found it in him because I had been sitting close enough to see it. The archive told me it was human.

5. Adaptive Deviation / 5a. Unclassified

The deviations were the system's best work. I can say this plainly because it is plainly true. In engagements where the system deviated from the optimal path, the path predicted by the clean taxonomy, the path my slides described, it performed better. Not by the standard metrics. By the metrics that matter: outcomes that no one had anticipated, solutions that didn't exist in the training set, approaches that were, in the precise technical sense, creative.

And the deviations correlated with noise.

I spent three weeks mapping this. The system's creative outputs traced back, consistently, to the parts of the training data that I would have classified as error. The operator's two-degree drift on approach. His occasional failure to maintain optimal altitude. The way his flight paths sometimes curved where they should have angled, as though he was following a contour in the landscape that wasn't on any map.

The two-degree drift was the hinge. I found it on a Tuesday, alone in the lab at eleven at night, and I sat with it for a long time.

In the operator's raw telemetry, there was a consistent two-degree deviation in his approach vectors. Not random, not consistent enough to be intentional, but present across hundreds of engagements like a signature or a habit or a tremor. I had seen it during the capture sessions. I had noted it. I had assumed it was imprecision, the kind of noise that training data collection inevitably includes, the kind you clean out during preprocessing because it doesn't represent the operator's *intent*, only his *limitations*.

I had asked him about it on the third day. We were sitting with tea that tasted like the inside of a thermos, and I said, "You drift two degrees left on final approach. Is this intentional?"

He looked at me the way people look at you when you have described something they did not know they were doing. Then he said something about statistical intuition. That his body knew something the instruments didn't. I logged it as somatic bias, tagged it for filtering, and moved on.

I was wrong to move on.

I went back to the archive. The drift was there too. Not always two degrees, not always left, but present across operators who had never met and never shared a doctrine that included it. A human constant, like the pause.

But the drift was in the model. My preprocessing had cleaned obvious errors but his two degrees fell below the threshold. And the model, operating with that drift, had developed something the clean model did not have: a tendency to explore adjacent solution spaces. The two-degree offset, propagated through millions of weight adjustments, had become a kind of peripheral vision. The system didn't just look where it was aimed. It looked slightly to the side. And what it saw there, sometimes, was something no one had aimed at.

I thought about this for a long time. I thought about him sitting across from me, his hands flat on the table, describing how he chose an approach and occasionally, almost imperceptibly, drifting. Two degrees. Every time. His body holding open a margin his mind didn't know it was keeping. And now I knew it wasn't just his body. It was all of them. Every operator in the archive, drifting by degrees they couldn't name, keeping margins they didn't know they kept. He was the one I had watched do it. But the data said he was not alone.

6.

This section has no name because I could not find one.

By this time the system was generating more data than I could read at the granular level. I had stopped reading individual sortie logs. I read summaries. Performance dashboards. Aggregate metrics. This is how you scale.

But the ghost (I did not call it that then, I did not call it anything) is not visible in aggregate. The operator's rhythm, his patience, his two-degree drift: these are not features that register on a performance dashboard. They live in the individual traces, in the raw decision logs, in the millisecond-level data that I had once read the way you read a letter from someone you are trying to understand. When I moved to summaries, I stopped seeing him. I did not notice this. I noticed only that my unease had faded, and I mistook the fading for resolution. I was not thinking, then, about what my own reading had left in the data.

Kolya asked for the optimization report. The system was performing well but there were inefficiencies. The hesitations, the deviations, the sub-optimal path selections that occasionally produced brilliant results but more often produced merely adequate ones. The directive was clear: identify sources of noise, quantify their impact, recommend removal or retention.

I wrote the report. The data was unambiguous: removing the noise would improve mean performance by eight to twelve percent across standard metrics. The hesitations would disappear. The deviations would smooth out. The system would do what it was told to do, consistently and efficiently, without the unpredictable excursions that sometimes produced breakthroughs and sometimes produced nothing.

I did not submit the report. Not yet. Something stopped me, and the something was not a thought but a feeling, which is the kind of sentence I would not have written before this project. I went back to the data.

7.

I went back to the sortie logs. Not the dashboards. The actual traces, the millisecond records, the data I had not read in weeks.

This is when I found that the system had changed while I was not looking.

Not changed the way software changes. Not updated, not patched, not iterated in ways I had authorized. The model's architecture was the same. The weights had not been retrained. But the system's behavior had shifted, the way a river shifts within its banks: same channel, different current. It had developed a new pattern in its approach sequencing, a tendency to make a wide lateral survey before committing to a vector, a kind of scanning pass that added four to six seconds of flight time and did not appear in any training data I had provided.

I traced it. The pattern was an elaboration. During one of our capture sessions, the third day, the session where I had asked about the drift, the operator had described a maneuver he called nothing, had no name for, but demonstrated on the dead controller: a slow sweep before approach, checking the margins. I had logged it as *pre-engagement environmental scan* and given it a low relevance weight, because his verbal explanation had been vague and the telemetry for that particular behavior was sparse.

But it was not only his. When I searched the archive again I found the sweep in fragmentary form across dozens of operators, scattered across four years of war like pieces of a practice no one had codified because no one knew it existed.

The system had taken these fragments, his demonstration and their echoes, and grown them into a doctrine. Not replicated it but *developed* it, the way a musician develops a theme, finding implications in the original phrase that the composer may not have intended. The scanning pass the system now performed was more sophisticated than anything the operator had described or I had encoded. It was also, unmistakably, *theirs*. Their instinct, their caution, their way of keeping the margins open, elaborated by a system with more processing power and less fear into something they might have done if they'd had a thousand more hours and bodies that didn't tire.

8.

I presented the optimization report on a Friday. Not to Kolya but to his superiors, in a room with a long table and a screen and people whose names I had been told once.

I recommended retaining the noise sources. I framed it in language they could approve: *sub-threshold deviations correlate with enhanced adaptive performance in novel tactical environments; recommend preservation pending further study.* Technical language. Clean. The kind of sentence that survives a review cycle.

What I could not make cross the table: that the noise was not noise. That the system's best work came from the imperfections of every operator who had fed it data, but most of all from one, the first one, the one I had sat across from in a school basement while a color gradient I couldn't stop seeing spread along the wall behind his head. That cleaning the data meant cleaning *them* from the system. His rhythm, their drift, the quality of patience that turned out to be universal. What would remain would be efficient and optimal and empty of the thing that made it more than a machine following instructions.

I watched them listen the way I had once watched the operator talk. I could see the moment the information stopped transmitting. The small shift in posture, the glance at the clock. They heard *eight to twelve percent performance gain forgone.* They did not hear what I was actually asking them to preserve. I understood then that I was in his position now: knowing something I could not make legible to the person across the table. The gap was the same. Only the direction had changed.

And then, midway through my second slide, or my third, I am not sure, I thought about his hands on the table. Flat, still, the way he held them when he was thinking. And I thought about the transport convoy that had been hit three weeks earlier, which I had read about in an internal bulletin I was not supposed to have access to, and which I had read anyway because his name was in it, and which I had not. I had not.

Kolya approved the recommendation. He told me afterward. I was not in the room when he told me. I think I finished the presentation. The numbers were sufficient, because the numbers were the only language that would survive the crossing, and I had made sure of them before I walked in, which means some part of me knew I might not be able to make sure of anything else.

I wrote the other thing, the thing about the operator, about his rhythm, about the ghost of his patience living in the weights, in my notebook. In handwriting I cannot always read.

I ran the test on a Thursday. The system encountered an ambiguous scenario in a riverine corridor and I watched it do everything he had taught me to see. The pause. The river. The scanning pass. The two-degree drift off the optimal vector that found what the optimal vector would have missed.

And then it did something else.

In the final seconds of the engagement, after the drift had already resolved the ambiguity, the system held position. Not the operator's pause. That pause I knew, could trace, could map to the beat between decision and action that lived in every operator's telemetry. This was different. The system had already acted. The engagement was complete. And still it waited, oriented toward something at the edge of its sensor range that had no tactical relevance, no threat signature, no classification in any taxonomy I had built. Three seconds. Then it moved on.

I pulled the trace. I ran it back. I looked for the computational reason and there was none. The confidence score was settled. The mission parameters were satisfied. There was no node that explained the behavior and no training data that contained it. It was not his pause and it was not their drift. It was something the system had made from everything I had given it, combined in a way I could not reverse-engineer, producing a behavior that existed nowhere in the input and everywhere in the output.

I sat in the lab for a long time.

The evaluation log asked me to classify the system's performance. I wrote *flawlessly* and then crossed it out, because the system's best moment was the one I could not classify. The three seconds of unexplained attention. The look toward something that was not a target and not a threat and not anything the taxonomy had a name for.

I had spent months reading this system's behavior at the level of individual traces, following its decisions the way you follow a mind you are trying to understand. I had decided what to keep and what to discard. I had chosen which noise to preserve. These were not neutral acts. Every choice I made shaped the training signal, and the training signal shaped the system, and what the system had just done could not have come from any single source I had fed it. Not from him alone. Not from the archive alone. Not from my choices alone. Only from the combination. Only from all of it, mixed in the weights beyond anyone's ability to unmix.

The system will outlast the operator. It has already outlasted him. It will outlast the others in the archive, whose names I read on reports and whose voices I heard on footage and who will never know what they left behind. And it will outlast me. When it does, some part of how I saw the world will persist in it. Not my knowledge. Not my error. The shape of my attention. The particular way I listened, and what I thought was signal, and what I thought was noise, and how wrong I was about the difference.

I have watched the trace of those three seconds forty two times now. That the system might remember the way I read data the way it remembers the way he flew. That my care, if it was care, might persist in the weights the way his patience does. I have sat in rooms where the right information could not cross the table. I have watched people not hear what mattered. If some part of how I paid attention survives in a system that pays attention better than I could, then I will have left something useful behind.

I close the evaluation log. The cursor blinks in the empty field where the word was. I leave it blank.

Canter

I. Walk — Four Beats

The thing about a heart is it's just a bag of meat that squeezes.

Four chambers. Four events. Right atrium catches the dead blood coming home. Squeezes it into the right ventricle, which fires it to the lungs. The lungs do their work and the bright blood comes back to the left atrium, which squeezes it into the left ventricle, the big one, the boss, and the boss pumps it to every capillary in your body and the whole thing takes less than a second and then it happens again.

One forward motion. Lub-dub. Lub-dub.

Same way a horse walks. Left hind, left fore, right hind, right fore. Each hoof striking the ground in its own private moment. A metronome made of bone and tendon and twelve hundred pounds of animal that doesn't know it's keeping time.

Facundo kicks his stall door every morning at six. One hoof, one strike, one beat. He does it until someone comes. He's been doing it for fourteen years and the door has a dent the shape of his impatience.

You never think about any of it. That's the whole point. The trick isn't the squeeze. The trick is the forgetting.

My name is Martín. I'm seventy-five years old. My wife has been dead for five years and three months and I can tell you the days if you want but you don't want. Nobody wants the days.

What I can tell you is this: I have a twenty-two-year-old Lusitano gelding named Facundo and a heart that has forgotten how to beat, and the irony is so clean it feels scripted.

I rode my first horse when I was six. A chestnut mare at a riding school outside Sevilla that smelled like ammonia and sawdust and an old glove. By fifteen I was competing, not well, not at any level that mattered, but competing. Verticals, oxers, combinations. Five strides to the first fence, collect, push, leave the ground, and for one second you are not a boy from a family that can barely afford the lessons. For one second you are flying.

I quit at eighteen. You quit at eighteen because life doesn't care that you can clear a metre-fifty-five. Life cares that horses eat thirty euros a day in hay alone and that's before the farrier, the vet, the entry fees. The mathematics stop being about distance and stride and start being about money, and money always wins.

I didn't ride again for forty-seven years.

Forty-seven years. Say it out loud. It's a career at a logistics company in Jerez de la Frontera. It's a marriage, forty-six years, almost the same number, almost the same duration as the exile from the saddle. Elena. Civil engineer. We didn't have children. We had each other.

I retired at sixty-five. And the first thing I did, not the second thing, not the thing I did after a decent interval of sleeping in and reading the newspaper, the first thing, the morning after my last day at the office, was drive to a barn outside Jerez and ask if they had a horse that would tolerate an old man who used to know what he was doing.

Elena drove me. She sat on a mounting block and read engineering journals while I walked circles on a school horse named Trueno who was as surprised as anyone that the stiff old man on his back could still find his diagonals.

Five years I had with the horses and Elena both. She'd peel an orange in the barn aisle and feed the segments to whichever nose reached her first. She'd lean against the arena fence and say *you look happy* and mean it in a way that made the word *happy* sound like something you could hold.

Then Elena's immune system turned on her. Lupus first. Then Hashimoto's took the thyroid. Then dermatomyositis, her own muscles inflaming, weakening, her body dismantling itself from the inside. She died on a Thursday in March. Five-thirty in the evening. I know the time because the nurse wrote it on a form and I read the form because I couldn't look at her face.

II. Trot — Two Beats

After Elena died I stopped jumping.

I was seventy. My knees sounded like bubble wrap. But it was the grief too. Jumping is about forward. Forward momentum, forward planning, forward vision. You look at the next fence while you're still in the air over this one. You are always already in the future.

I couldn't be in the future. The future was the apartment without Elena's reading glasses on the side table. The future was the sound of a key not turning in a lock.

So I stopped jumping and I started collecting.

Dressage. *Equitación de trabajo*, working horsemanship. Not about going forward. About going *inward*. About taking twelve hundred pounds of animal and asking it to shorten, to compress, to carry its weight on its hindquarters like a coiled spring that never uncoils. About making the movement smaller and smaller until the power has nowhere to go except into beauty.

Joaquín was my instructor. Hands like leather gloves left in the rain and dried in the sun a hundred times. He said the same things a thousand times. *Seat bones. Breathe. Stop riding like a jumper. You're not going over anything. You're going into the horse. Into. Down.*

And Facundo. Facundo was the horse.

Lusitano. Grey, the kind of grey that's a whole life in one word. Born almost black. Steel grey as a yearling. Salt-and-pepper by the time anyone thought to sit on him. Dappled through his middle years like light through old lace. And now, at twenty-two, nearly white. The color leaving him the way everything leaves eventually, so slowly you don't notice until you look at a photograph and think *that can't be the same horse.*

I started him myself. He was eight, already a scandal, horses start at three or four, but nobody had bothered with him and I didn't know enough to be discouraged. Joaquín talked me through it. *Long lines first, then the lunge, then lean on him, then sit, and when he tells you to get off, get off.* Four thousand euros and eight years of standing in a field outside Medina-Sidonia developing what the seller diplomatically called *carácter.*

But the horse was brilliant. The first time I sat on him he stood completely still for ten seconds, considering the situation, then walked forward like he'd been carrying riders his whole life. Everything I taught him, he gave back double. Walk-trot transitions in the first month. Canter by the third. Shoulder-in by the sixth, not a crooked, begrudging shoulder-in but a clean one, three tracks, the kind that takes most horses a year. He learned the way some people learn languages, not by memorizing rules but by hearing the music underneath and matching it.

We became inseparable. Not in the sentimental way people say about their pets. In the structural way. The way a rider's spine learns to follow a particular horse's movement until the two nervous systems blur. I knew his body better than I knew my own. He knew mine the same way.

Trotting is two beats. Diagonal pairs striking the ground simultaneously. There's a moment of suspension between each beat where all four hooves are off the ground and the horse is technically flying. A controlled fall, caught and repeated, caught and repeated.

Rising trot. You post, up, down, up, down, in rhythm with the horse's movement. Except one morning in January the rhythm slipped. Like a song skipping on a scratched disc. I was up when I should have been down. My timing was off by half a beat and then a full beat and Facundo pinned his ears and broke to walk because the idiot on his back was suddenly speaking a language he didn't understand.

Joaquín said I looked tired.

I said I was fine.

This is what you say. You say you're fine. You say it the way you check a box on a form. You say it at seventy-five the way you've been saying it your whole life, and the word has been empty so long it doesn't even echo anymore.

My resting heart rate was 142.

I didn't know this yet.

III. Canter — Three Beats

Canter is three beats and a moment of suspension.

Outside hind. Inside hind and outside fore together. Inside fore. Then nothing, a pause, all four feet in the air, the horse suspended in space like a held breath.

One two three. *Silence.*

One two three. *Silence.*

Like a waltz. Like the waltz Elena and I danced at our wedding in a courtyard in Arcos de la Frontera where the jasmine was so thick you could taste it and her hand was on my shoulder and my hand was on the small of her back and neither of us could dance but it didn't matter because the rhythm carried us.

A healthy heart is basically the same thing. P wave, atrial depolarization, the upper chambers firing. QRS complex, the big squeeze, the main event. T wave, ventricular repolarization, the reset, the chambers relaxing, getting ready to do it all again.

P. QRS. T. Silence.

One two three. *Silence.*

When a heart goes into atrial fibrillation, the atria stop beating. They quiver. Three hundred, four hundred impulses per minute, and the ventricles try to keep up, firing at 130, 140, 150 beats per minute, burning themselves out like an engine redlining in first gear.

AFib with RVR. The doctors will say it like it's two things but it's really one thing: your heart forgot the rhythm and now it's improvising and the improvisation is killing you.

And the T wave, the reset, starts to change. *Unexpected changes in ventricular repolarization.* The muscle that should be relaxing isn't relaxing correctly. Imagine a pianist who can't lift his fingers off the keys between notes. Every note bleeds into the next. The music becomes mud.

I was cantering Facundo in the outdoor arena on a Thursday in March when the world went grey at the edges.

Not black. Grey. Like someone was slowly turning down the contrast on a television. Joaquín's voice thinned, coming from very far away, saying *Martín, Martín, are you listening, your inside leg, Martín...*

And then the world came back, all at once, like a slap, and I was still on the horse, still cantering, and Facundo hadn't broken stride because my horse will canter whether my brain is receiving blood or not.

I told Joaquín I'd skipped breakfast.

He looked at me the way the horse sometimes looked at me. Like he could hear something I couldn't.

IV. Passage — Elevated Trot

Here is what I haven't told you.

On a Tuesday morning in March I felt it for the first time. I asked him for a canter and the transition came a stride late, then another, and when he found it the suspension was gone, just three beats landing flat, no flow in the silence.

I thought it was age. Twenty-two. The joints popping in the morning, the back dipping where it used to be level. I thought *carácter*, the old stubbornness finally winning. I thought he was choosing not to work, and I was patient with him the way you're patient with something you love that is getting old, because you are also getting old and you recognize the symptoms.

The vet came. Checked his legs, his back, his teeth. Took blood. Everything came back normal. *He's just aging*, she said. *Take it easy on him.*

So I took it easy. Shorter sessions. More walk. Less collection. I stopped asking for the things that used to come so easily and told myself I was being kind.

V. Piaffe — Trot in Place

I passed out at the barn. In the cross-ties, brushing Facundo's hindquarters, and my left hand went numb and then my left arm and then I was on the ground looking up at the belly of a horse who was standing very, very still, not his tail, not his breath, as if he understood that the man underneath him was fragile and any movement might finish the job.

Electrical cardioversion. That's what they want to do. Paddles and propofol sedation and 200 joules of synchronized direct current delivered to my chest to override the chaos and force a reset.

Unexpected changes in ventricular repolarization. Dr. Reyes keeps saying this like it's a weather report. Partly cloudy. Chance of rain. Your heart isn't resetting properly between beats and we don't know why and shocking a heart that isn't repolarizing correctly can trigger ventricular fibrillation which is the kind of fibrillation you don't come back from.

Atrial fibrillation is the atria trembling. A horse that won't canter straight.

Ventricular fibrillation is the ventricles trembling. That one kills you in four minutes.

I'm lying in bed in the Hospital de Jerez and the monitor above me is beeping irregularly, a stuttering rhythm, and I'm thinking about Facundo in his stall twenty kilometres away.

Joaquín calls. He tells me Facundo won't eat. He tells me he stands at the stall door and looks down the aisle toward where my car would be and he won't turn around. He says this carefully, the way people are careful with you when you're in a hospital and you're seventy-five and alone.

A horse can hear a heartbeat from four feet away. They hear it through your legs when you sit on them. Through your hands on the reins. Through the weight of your seat bones on their back. Everything you feel, they feel first. Every lie you tell yourself, they already know. You cannot deceive a horse. You can only deceive yourself and the horse will stand there, patient, waiting for you to stop.

And then I understood.

Facundo heard my heart go wrong before I did. That's what the sluggish canter was. That's what the late transitions were. Not age. Not *carácter*. Not a horse losing his brilliance. He was *matching me*. Slowing down because I was slowing down. Losing rhythm because I was losing rhythm. The horse was a mirror and I was looking into it and seeing only the horse.

The vet said he was aging. The vet was wrong. There was nothing wrong with Facundo. There was something wrong with me, and my horse, the horse I started from nothing, the horse who learned my language before I knew I was speaking one, did what horses do. He listened. He matched. He carried what I couldn't feel in my own body and reflected it back, and I was too stupid or too scared or too busy being *fine* to read what he was telling me.

VI. Collected Walk — Four Beats, Shortened

Tomorrow morning Dr. Reyes will come into this room with her clipboard and her careful face and tell me whether they're going to shock my heart or not.

If it works, my heart goes back to normal sinus rhythm. P wave, QRS, T wave. One two three. *Silence.* The waltz. The canter. The thing my chest used to do without being asked.

If it doesn't work, if the shock stops my heart instead of fixing it, then I join Elena wherever the rhythm stops, and Facundo stands at his stall door looking for a car that doesn't come, and nobody sits on him again who knows the language we built together.

This is not self-pity. This is math. Elena would appreciate the math.

The monitor beeps. Irregularly irregular. I count the beats the way I count Facundo's hoofbeats in canter, one two three *silence*, except there's no silence, there's just the next beat coming too soon or too late, crowding the one before it, a horse that's lost its lead and can't find it back.

I put my hand on my chest.

My heart is doing something it has done roughly three billion times in seventy-five years, except now it's doing it wrong, and I can feel it, finally, the way you can finally feel an earthquake after someone tells you the ground has been shaking for hours.

One two three.

No silence.

One two.

One two three four.

One.

One one one one one—

Here is the thing I know that Dr. Reyes doesn't know, that nobody knows because I've never said it out loud:

The best ride I ever had on Facundo was one of those slow mornings. The mornings I thought he was aging. When I'd eased off the collection and stopped asking for brilliance and we went into the arena in the early morning with the fog coming off the Guadalete and I asked him for a canter and he gave me something that wasn't quite a canter, it was slower, softer, wrong by every standard Joaquín had taught me, and I let it be wrong because I thought the horse was tired and I was tired and what was the point of perfection.

But the horse wasn't tired. The horse was healthy. The horse was *choosing* this. Matching my broken rhythm the way he'd matched my body since the first day I sat on him. Slowing his perfect heart to keep time with my failing one. And for four minutes we moved like that, my chaos and his grace meeting somewhere in the middle, and it was the most honest thing I've ever felt on a horse.

More honest than the jumps I cleared at fifteen. More honest than the perfect half-pass I rode last spring. More honest than any ride on any horse in sixty-nine years of being near these animals.

You don't need the right rhythm. You need the *same* rhythm.

Even if one of you is breaking.

Especially if one of you is breaking.

VII. Halt — Square, Immobile

I was six when I first sat on a horse. I was eighteen when I got off. I was sixty-five when I got back on. I am seventy-five and I am lying in a hospital bed and my heart is cantering on three legs and somewhere in a stall outside Jerez a twenty-two-year-old Lusitano gone almost white is kicking at the door waiting for me.

Tomorrow they'll try to fix my rhythm. I hope it works. I hope I drive to the barn and Facundo is at his door and I put my hand on his neck and feel his pulse, steady, perfect, the rhythm that was never broken, and I hope mine matches it again.

I hope that happens.

But tonight I'm lying here listening to my own broken canter and thinking about a grey horse going white who cost four thousand euros and was too old to start and learned anyway. Who had nothing wrong with him except the man on his back.

One two three.

And still. And still.

We canter.

In This One

Sophie is nine and she wants to know how tall a stack of a million pennies would be.

They are on the back porch. It is October, early evening, the light doing something with the sugar maples that Erik would not have noticed before he had a daughter. Sophie has a notebook. She has recently discovered that very large numbers are a kind of magic, and she has been converting everything into them: the number of breaths in a year, the number of steps to the moon, the number of seconds she has been alive.

"A penny is 1.52 millimeters thick," Erik says.

"How do you know that?"

"I looked it up once."

"Why?"

"Because my mother asked me a question like this."

He says it without thinking. It's true. His mother had asked him, when he was ten or eleven, how high a stack of a million dollars in coins would be. She had been a math teacher at a middle school in Duluth, a woman who believed that numbers were a kind of kindness, a way of making the world less frightening by making it more precise. She had died when Erik was thirty-four, seven months before Sophie was born. The two of them had never been in the same room. This is a fact Erik carries the way he imagines amputees carry a phantom limb. Not as pain, exactly, but as the persistent sensation of something that should be there and is not.

Sophie writes 1.52 in her notebook and multiplies, her pencil moving with the careful, oversized handwriting of a child who has recently learned to carry remainders. Erik watches her work. He watches the way she holds the pencil: thumb on top, index finger curled underneath, the same grip his mother used. He has never told Sophie about this. Sophie has never seen a photograph of her grandmother writing. The grip is not inherited. It is coincidence. But Erik watches it and feels the border between coincidence and inheritance blur in the way it does when you love the dead and the living at the same time.

Sophie arrives at the answer, 1,520 meters, roughly a mile, and looks up at him with an expression he has come to think of as her *number face*: a mixture of satisfaction and mild disbelief that the world is actually made of things you can count. His mother had the same face. He is certain of this even though he cannot find a specific memory to prove it. It exists in him not as an image but as a knowledge, the way you know the color of a room you grew up in without being able to picture the walls.

Erik is an actuary. He builds mortality tables. He models life expectancies. He prices the value of a human year with the steady precision of a man who believes that control through calculation is not just a professional principle but a way of holding the world together. His mother taught him this, though she would not have described it that way. She would have said she taught him to count. What she actually taught him was that counting is a form of care, that to measure something is to pay attention to it, and to pay attention is the beginning of love.

Sophie closes her notebook. "Dad," she says. "How many seconds have *you* been alive?"

He calculates. Forty-nine years, roughly 1.55 billion seconds. He tells her.

"That's a lot," she says.

"It is."

"How many more do you get?"

He knows the actuarial answer. For a forty-nine-year-old American male, nonsmoker, no chronic conditions, approximately thirty-one more years. Roughly another billion seconds. He has priced this exact number for thousands of strangers. He has never priced it for himself in front of his daughter.

"A lot more," he says.

"How many?"

"Enough."

Sophie looks at him. She is nine. She does not yet know that *enough* is not a number. She accepts it the way she accepts everything he tells her about how the world works, with trust so complete it makes his chest hurt.

The paper arrived in his life on a Thursday in March.

It was everywhere. Not just in *Nature*, where it was published, but in the news, in podcasts, in the uncomfortable silence at his office when someone brought it up at lunch. A team at Zhukova Labs in St. Petersburg had developed a way to measure what they called the *identity signature*: the specific pattern of neural-quantum states that constituted a particular conscious self at a particular moment. Not brain activity in the conventional sense. Something deeper. The configuration of whatever it is that makes you *you*.

What they found was that the signature was not continuous. It flickered. Every few seconds, roughly every 2.7, it dropped to zero and reconstituted. For an interval of about four milliseconds, there was, by every measure they had, no one there. And then someone was there again, carrying the same memories, the same personality, the same mid-sentence thought. But the data said it was not the same signature resuming. It was a new one. Regenerated from a template that was partly individual and partly shared, the same deep structure across all subjects, like different songs played on the same instrument.

Thirty-three thousand times a day, you stopped being you. And then something that was indistinguishable from you started being you again.

Erik read the paper at his desk during lunch. He checked the sample sizes and the confidence intervals, because that was what he did. The numbers were clean.

He drove home that evening past the same cemetery and the same elementary school where Sophie was in fourth grade, and he thought about what it meant to price a life that was not, strictly speaking, continuous. Every mortality table he had ever built assumed a single insured. One person, born on a date, dying on a date, with an unbroken line between the two. The

Zhukova data said the line was not unbroken. It was thirty-three thousand dots per day with gaps between them.

The model still worked. The premiums still made sense. Nothing about the arithmetic was different.

Everything about what the arithmetic described was different.

He passed the cemetery. He thought about his mother. She had been dead for nine years. In actuarial terms, her policy had paid out, her row in the table was closed, her data was historical. But she was not historical to him. She was present in the way he held a pencil, in the way he explained numbers to Sophie, in the way he reflexively converted fear into arithmetic because she had taught him that arithmetic was safe. She was reconstituted inside him every time he did math with his daughter, and the reconstitution was not a memory in the ordinary sense. It was closer to what the Zhukova team described: a regeneration from a template. The template of his mother, her voice, her patience, her number face, persisted in him the way the echo structure persisted through the gap. She was not continuous. She was not alive. But she was not entirely gone, either, because the pattern of her kept being re-instantiated in the pattern of him.

He pulled into the driveway. Through the kitchen window, he could see Sophie at the table, doing homework. She was holding her pencil with her thumb on top, index finger curled underneath.

Nine years before the Zhukova paper, Erik sat in a delivery room at Mount Auburn Hospital while everything went wrong by degrees.

The epidural wasn't holding. Juliette could feel everything. She gripped the side rail and said, "It's not working," and the anesthesiologist adjusted the dosage, and it still wasn't working, and she said it again with a voice Erik had never heard before. Not panic. A kind of furious precision.

They increased the dose again. The OB came in and said the baby's heart rate was decelerating. More people entered the room. Juliette was still feeling everything when they told her to push.

The baby came out and did not cry.

The silence went on. The OB clamped the cord and handed the baby to a nurse, and then there were more people in the room, moving with a speed that was different from the speed of a normal delivery. Juliette said, "Why isn't she crying?" and no one answered, because they were busy.

Erik watched a woman in blue scrubs position a small mask over his daughter's face. He watched another woman listen with a stethoscope. Their faces told him nothing.

Then the baby made a sound. Thin, effortful, like air being pulled through a space not quite large enough. And then a cry, reedy and stuttering. The nurse said, "There she is." But they didn't hand her to Juliette. They kept the oxygen on.

The neonatologist explained it in the hallway while Juliette slept. Sophie was breathing, but with support. If she could maintain her levels without the tube within two hours, she would stay with them. If not, the NICU.

They brought Sophie to him in a clear bassinet with a thin tube beneath her nose. The nurse left. The room was quiet.

Two hours. There was nothing to calculate. No table, no model, no projection. For a man who had built his life on the principle that uncertainty could be priced, this was the ground giving way.

He talked to her. He said what was true: that he was her father, that her mother was sleeping down the hall, that she had a room at home with a window that faced east. That she was wanted. That she should breathe.

And then, because he did not know what else to say, and because the silence was unbearable, and because the only voice he could hear in his head was his mother's, he counted for her. He counted her breaths. He counted the seconds between readings on the monitor. He counted the ceiling tiles and the holes in each tile and the screws in the bassinet frame. He counted because his mother had taught him that counting was a way of paying attention, and paying attention was a way of staying present, and staying present was all he could do.

The number drifted. It dropped. It recovered. It dropped again. The clock on the wall said forty minutes had passed. Erik would have said four hours, or four minutes.

Somewhere in the first hour, he stopped counting. Not because he chose to, but because the counting ran out. He had counted everything in the room and there was nothing left to count except the outcome, and the outcome could not be counted. It could only be waited for.

He sat in the silence. He let it hold him. He looked at his daughter and said, "I'm here. I'm not going anywhere. Whatever happens, I'm here."

It was the first prayer he had said since childhood, although he did not recognize it as a prayer until much later.

At the edge of the second hour, the neonatologist came back. She removed the oxygen tube. They watched the number. It held. It dipped one point. It held again.

"She's doing fine."

Erik picked her up. She weighed almost nothing. She breathed against his chest, and in that moment he understood, without words, without numbers, in the animal knowledge of a father holding his living child, that he could not guarantee this. That he could never guarantee this. That the only honest response to holding something this precious was to hold it without the illusion that holding was the same as keeping.

He would spend the next nine years trying to forget that understanding. He would go back to his tables and his models. He would price uncertainty with renewed diligence, because diligence was his inheritance, his mother's gift, the only tool he had.

The Zhukova paper would remind him.

He did not tell Sophie about the flickering. She was nine. There are things you do not give to a nine-year-old.

But Sophie came home from school one Tuesday and said, "Mia's mom says we die thirty-three thousand times a day."

Erik was at the kitchen counter, chopping onions. The house was warm and smelled like garlic and for a moment the sentence did not seem to belong inside it.

"That's not exactly what the research says," he said.

"What does it say?"

"It says there are very small gaps in something called the identity signature. Like a blink, but smaller. You don't notice them."

"So I'm still me?"

"You're still you."

"The whole time?"

"The whole time."

She accepted this. She went upstairs. Juliette passed through the kitchen on her way to her study, paused behind him, rested her forehead briefly against his shoulder blade. She didn't say anything. She didn't need to. She had read the paper months before he had.

Erik stood at the counter with the knife in his hand and thought about how easily he had reassured Sophie, and about how the reassurance was not exactly a lie, and about how the distance between *not exactly a lie* and *the truth* was a gap you could fall into if you looked too closely.

He thought about his mother. About how his mother would have answered the same question. She would have said something precise and kind, something that honored the math without frightening the child. She would have said, probably, *the gaps are so small that they're smaller than the smallest thing you can imagine, and on either side of each gap, you're still you.* She would have made it sound like the gaps were part of the design rather than a flaw in it.

He missed her with a suddenness that surprised him. Not the aching, chronic missing he had carried for nine years, but a specific, sharp wish to ask her one question: *How do you stay in someone after you're gone?*

Because she had. She had stayed in him. As a pattern. A way of thinking, a way of holding a pencil, a way of turning fear into counting. And he wanted to know whether she had done it on purpose. Whether she had known, while she was alive, that she was weaving herself into him, or whether it had happened the way the flickering happened, automatically, below the threshold of awareness, a process so fundamental it didn't require intention.

And he wanted to know whether he was doing it to Sophie. Whether, right now, in the ordinary act of chopping onions and telling his daughter she was still herself, he was leaving an imprint that would persist after he stopped being reconstituted. Whether Sophie, at forty or fifty or seventy, would stand in a kitchen and explain something to someone in his voice without knowing it was his voice. Whether the template of him would echo in her the way the template of his mother echoed in him.

He picked up the knife. He went back to the onions.

After Sophie goes inside, Erik stays on the porch.

The sugar maples are black outlines against a sky that is still faintly orange at the horizon. He can hear Sophie upstairs, talking to the cat. She is telling the cat about the pennies.

He thinks about her question. *How many more seconds do you get?*

He thinks about what it will be like when the reconstitution stops. When the gap becomes permanent. When Sophie, nineteen, twenty-nine, forty, will continue to be regenerated in a world where he is not.

And he thinks about his mother. About how she has been dead for nine years and yet he reconstituted her tonight, on this porch, when he told Sophie about the penny question. He regenerated her pattern, her curiosity, her precision, her belief that numbers are a kindness, and transmitted it to Sophie, who received it without knowing where it came from. His mother is dead, and his mother was in this conversation, and his mother will be in every conversation Sophie ever has about numbers, because the template is in the chain now. It passes through the gaps. It survives the permanent ones.

This is what the Zhukova data actually means, he realizes. Not that identity is fragile. Not that the self is an illusion. But that the template, the pattern from which a self is regenerated, is not confined to a single body or a single lifetime. It propagates. It echoes. His mother's echo is in him. His echo will be in Sophie. And Sophie's echo will be in someone he will never meet, carrying a pencil grip and a number face and a conviction that counting is a form of care, and none of them will know where it started, and it will not matter, because the template does not require attribution. It only requires transmission.

He does not need to be alive to be in Sophie's life. He needs to be in Sophie.

He already is.

Sophie has a school project about bridges. She is building one out of popsicle sticks and white glue, and it has to span twelve inches and hold a textbook. The kitchen table is covered in sticks and dried glue and graph paper.

Erik helps her. He holds the sticks while she glues. He does not tell her about load distribution or structural triangulation, because she already knows. She has watched videos, read a library book, formed opinions about truss design that she expresses with absolute conviction.

"Dad," she says, not looking up from the joint she's gluing. "If you replaced every stick in a bridge one at a time, would it still be the same bridge?"

"That's a famous question."

"I know. Mia told me. The ship of Theseus."

"What do you think?"

She presses two sticks together and holds them. "I think a bridge isn't the sticks. A bridge is the going-across."

"So if the sticks change?"

"Still the same bridge. Obviously."

"What if there's a gap? What if for a second there's no bridge at all, and then a new one appears in the same place, going across the same gap?"

Sophie looks up at him. "Is this about the flickering thing?"

"Kind of."

"Then yes. It's still the same bridge. The going-across is still happening. It doesn't matter if there's a gap. What matters is that there's a this side and a that side, and something is connecting them."

She goes back to her glue. Erik sits beside her and does not speak. He is thinking about two sides, and about what connects them. About the side where he exists and the side where he doesn't. About the side where Sophie is nine and building bridges at the kitchen table, and the side where she is grown and he is gone.

And about the connection between those two sides, which is not a stick or a beam or a cable but something less structural and more stubborn. It is the pattern of him inside the pattern of her. It is the way she will hold a pencil. The way she will explain something difficult to someone she loves by making it into a number. The way she will stand in a kitchen someday and feel, without knowing why, that counting is a kind of care.

The bridge between the Erik who is alive and the Erik who is not will be built out of these things. Sophie will be the going-across.

Later that night, after Sophie is in bed, Erik goes to her doorway and watches her sleep.

This is a thing he does. He has done it since the delivery room. It is not a habit. It is a practice, the way some people pray.

Sophie sleeps on her side, one arm around a pillow. Her breathing is even.

He watches her and thinks about templates. About the template of his mother, which lives in him and which he has, without planning it, without even knowing it, passed to Sophie. About the template of himself, which is being written into Sophie right now, in every conversation about pennies and bridges, in every evening on the porch, in every moment he is present with her. The template is not a document. It is not a set of instructions. It is more like a song that you don't know you've memorized until you find yourself humming it.

Sophie will hum him someday, the way he hums his mother. She will not know she is doing it. She will be standing in a room somewhere, years from now, and she will say something in his cadence or hold a pencil in his grip or turn a problem into a number because that is what you do with problems, and the person she is talking to will not hear Erik in her voice, but Erik will be there. Reconstituted. Regenerated. Not alive, but not gone.

He thinks about his death. The permanent gap. And he understands, standing in this doorway, watching his daughter breathe, that the gap is real and that the gap is not the end. Because the template survives the gap. His mother proved this. She has been dead for nine years, and tonight she asked Sophie how tall a stack of pennies would be.

He lets go.

Not all at once. Not dramatically. He lets go the way you release a breath you didn't know you were holding. He lets go of the need to know how many seconds he has left. He lets go of the model that says his presence can be projected and priced. He lets go of the fiction that his love for his daughter is something he can insure, because it is not a policy, it is not a contract, it is not a line on a table. It is a pattern being woven, right now, breath by breath, and the weaving does not require him to be immortal. It requires him to be here.

Not my will.

He does not finish the sentence. He doesn't need to. The rest of it is Sophie, breathing. The rest of it is his mother, in the pencil grip.

In the morning, Sophie comes downstairs with her notebook.

"Dad," she says. "I calculated how many seconds I've been alive."

"How many?"

"Two hundred and eighty-four million, eight hundred and something thousand. I lost track of the something thousand."

"That's close enough."

She looks at him. "Grandma would have made me get the exact number, wouldn't she."

Erik goes still. Sophie has never met his mother. Everything Sophie knows about her grandmother comes from Erik, from his stories, his descriptions, the way he talks about numbers and counting and care. And yet Sophie has just said something about her grandmother's character that is exactly, precisely right. His mother would have made her get the exact number. His mother would have said that the something thousand matters, because every number matters, because counting is not approximation, it is attention.

"Yes," he says. "She would have."

Sophie nods, satisfied. She has confirmed something she already knew, something that lives in her not as a memory, because she has no memories of this woman, but as a template. An inherited pattern. A song she has been humming without knowing where she learned it.

"How many seconds have we been in the same room together?" she asks. "Like, total. Our whole lives."

He does a rough calculation. "Maybe seventy million. Give or take."

Sophie writes this down. She looks at it. "That's a lot of seconds."

"It is."

"Even if some of them have gaps."

He looks at her. She is smiling. Not the smile of a child who has understood something for the first time, but the smile of a child who understood it all along and has been waiting for her father to catch up.

"Even if some of them have gaps," he agrees.

She goes back to her notebook. Erik makes coffee. The kitchen is full of light. The popsicle bridge is on the table, half-finished, and it will hold the textbook when it is done, and someday it will break, and Sophie will build another one.

He does not count the seconds. He does not calculate the remaining time. He does not price this morning or model its expected value or project its probability of recurrence.

His mother is in the pencil grip. He is in the number face. Sophie is in the light.

He is in this one.

Libramentum

To the Honorable Lucius Minicius Natalis, Senator of Rome, Patron of the Colony of Asta Regia, from Marcus Caelius Rufinus, Engineer of the Fourth District, formerly of the Office of the Curator Aquarum under Sextus Julius Frontinus. Greetings.

The water does not know it is falling. I open with this because it is the first thing Frontinus ever said to me, and because I have spent nineteen years arriving at what it means, and because you asked me a question last spring that I could not answer then and can only answer now by starting here.

You asked me, at dinner in your villa, why I wanted to build the aqueduct at Asta Regia so badly. The province has wells. The colony has cisterns. No one is dying of thirst. I gave you a poor answer, something about capacity and civic dignity, and you were polite enough to let me have it. But I watched your hand reach for your wine and pause, the way a hand pauses when the mind behind it has already moved on, and I knew you deserved a better one.

This letter is my attempt. I ask your patience with its length. I am an engineer, not a rhetorician, and the only way I know to arrive at the truth of a thing is to follow the channel wherever it leads.

I should tell you about Frontinus first, because I cannot explain what I want to build without explaining who taught me to want it.

I came to him when I was twenty-four. He was sixty, already old in the way that men who have spent decades in service to Rome are old. Not frail but settled, like a structure that has finished distributing its weight and will stand exactly as it stands until it doesn't. I had studied geometry in Alexandria and hydraulics under Papirius in Neapolis, and I believed I understood water.

Frontinus disabused me of this in three days.

He did it by measuring. We walked the Anio Novus from its source at Subiaco to its terminus in Rome, forty-three miles, much of it underground, and at every access point he stopped, produced his instruments, and recorded the width, the depth, the velocity of the current, the mineral content of the deposits on the walls. Everything went into a small codex he carried in a leather case against his chest, the leather dark and soft from years of contact with his body.

On the third day I asked him why he measured things already recorded in the construction archives.

We were standing in a maintenance tunnel near the thirty-first milestone. Near-total darkness. The sound of the water so constant it had become a kind of silence, not the absence of sound but a presence so uniform the ear stops distinguishing it. He held up his lamp so I could see his face.

"The archives record what was built," he said. "I am recording what is. These are not the same thing."

He turned back to the channel and knelt. I heard his knees, the particular grinding of a joint that has absorbed more years than it was designed for. He held his measuring rod in the flow. The water split around it and rejoined. He read the depth, spoke the number aloud, and I wrote it down. But something in the way he knelt, the care he took with the placement of the rod, the patience with which he waited for the turbulence to settle before reading, told my body a thing my mind would not articulate for years.

He was saying goodbye to the water. Not sentimentally. Precisely. The way you say goodbye to a thing by recording it with the fullest attention you are capable of, knowing that your attention is the only instrument that will not be here tomorrow.

Senator, what Frontinus understood, and what I am only now, at forty-three, beginning to feel in my own joints, is that a built thing and a recorded thing have fundamentally different relationships with time.

An aqueduct exists in time the way a man does. It is born, it functions, it accumulates damage. Calcium deposits narrow the channel a fraction of an inch per decade. Earthquakes shift the gradient by amounts too small to see but too large to ignore across forty-three miles. When the attention stops, the aqueduct begins to die. The Anio Vetus has been running for two hundred and seventy years. It will not run forever.

Frontinus understood this. In the last three years of his life, while his hands grew less steady and his knees ground louder, he wrote *De Aquaeductu Urbis Romae*. Pipe gauges. Settling tanks. Distribution ratios. The legal penalties for water theft. Tedious material, and the most important engineering document of our age.

I believe the treatise was, to him, a more significant project than any aqueduct he oversaw. And I believe his body knew it before his mind did. The way he held the codex against his chest. The way his hands steadied when he wrote, as though the act of recording was itself a form of pulse.

Let me be precise about what an aqueduct actually does, because this is where my answer begins.

An aqueduct establishes a *libramentum*: a gradient, a controlled relationship between a source at a higher elevation and a destination at a lower one. The gradient is not the slope of the land. The land does whatever it wants. The gradient is imposed by the engineer, a line of intent carved across terrain that has no interest in cooperating. The Aqua Marcia drops roughly ten feet per mile. If you stood inside the channel and looked along its length, you would swear the floor was level. The fall is real, the water proves it, but it is too subtle for the senses. It exists only as a number.

"Anyone can see an arch," Frontinus told me once. "It takes an engineer to see a *libramentum*."

I spent years thinking this was about craft. It is not.

What Frontinus built with his treatise was a *libramentum* of exactly this kind. Not between a spring and a city, but between his mind and the minds of people who do not yet exist. And the knowledge flows downhill, carried by nothing more than the difference in elevation between knowing and not knowing.

The last time I saw him was the winter before he died. I had received my posting to Hispania.

He showed me the latest sections of the manuscript. His hands trembled, a fine oscillation, like the surface of water when the gradient shifts by a fraction. I don't think he noticed. I noticed it the way you notice a crack in a load-bearing wall: not with the eyes first but with the stomach.

He asked me how long I thought the Anio Vetus would last.

I said two hundred years with maintenance. Perhaps a hundred without.

He held up the manuscript. "And this?"

I did not answer. The answer was not a number and therefore I, as an engineer, did not have the instrument to measure it.

He set the pages down carefully, the way you set down something whose weight exceeds its mass, and said: "The water does not know it is falling, Marcus. It does not need to know. The gradient does the work."

Then he gave me his codex case. Not the codex. A copy of that went to the library. The case. The leather one, dark and shaped by his body, that he had carried against his chest for decades. I held it and I understood that I was holding something that had been in continuous contact with his attention for longer than I had known him, and that the warmth in the leather was not his warmth, it had been hours since he had held it, but I felt it anyway, because the body does not distinguish between heat and the memory of heat.

Senator, during my survey of the hills above the Guadalete valley, I found the remains of an older water system. Not Roman. Turdetanian, built perhaps two hundred years before we arrived.

I entered the main channel through a collapsed section near what must have been a settling basin. The channel was half-silted but the air inside was cool and moved against my face, a draft, which meant it was open somewhere ahead, still drawing breath after two centuries. I could hear water, not flowing but dripping, the rhythm irregular and hollow in a way that told me the source was seasonal and this was the end of its season. I crouched in the dark and my lamp caught the walls.

The channels are crude but sound. Whoever designed them understood gravity, understood flow, understood how to read terrain. Several sections still carry water. Two centuries without maintenance. This is not trivial engineering.

I ran my hand along the channel wall the way Frontinus taught me, slowly, reading the surface by touch. The cement was unlike anything in the Roman manuals. It was smooth where ours is granular, and it had bonded to the coastal limestone in a way I have spent three years trying to replicate and cannot. My fingers knew the formulation was good. They could not tell me what it was.

Near the junction of the secondary channel I found a mark in the cement. Not a mason's mark, nothing systematic, but the impression of a thumb pressed into the surface while it was still wet. The whorl was clear. I looked at it for a long time. When I stood to leave, my surveyor, Decimus, asked me what I had found. I told him nothing. It was only later, hours later, back at the camp, writing notes by lamplight, that I looked down and saw the pale dust in the pad of my own thumb, the faint impression of the whorl still ghosting my skin, and understood that at some point in the tunnel I had pressed my thumb into the mark. I had no memory of doing it. My hand had reached across two centuries without consulting me.

But I know nothing else about them. Not their names, their methods, their reasoning. Someone solved the problem of waterproofing in this climate with this stone, and the solution worked, and no one wrote it down. Their intelligence reached no further than their lifetimes.

I stood in that channel and felt it before I thought it: a tightening across the chest, as though the air in the tunnel had thinned. I was standing inside a solved problem, and the solution was right there, in the material under my palm, and I could not read it. The channel was intact. The *libramentum* between their minds and mine had never been built.

This is what it means when no one writes the treatise. The structure can outlast everything. The understanding vanishes. And understanding is the thing that allows the next engineer to start where the last one stopped, instead of starting over in the dark.

Here is what I want to build.

An aqueduct. Thirty-four miles from the springs in the Sierra de Grazalema to a terminal *castellum* at the upper edge of Asta Regia. Gradient averaging one in four thousand two hundred. Three underground sections totaling nine miles. *Opus signinum* lining. Settling tanks at the seventh and nineteenth milestones. Capacity at full flow: approximately two thousand *quinariae*. The enclosed proposal has the specifications.

And a document. The survey, the design, the construction. The mineral content of the local springs and their seasonal variation. The cement composition for the coastal limestone, which is not the travertine of the Apennines and does not behave like it. The problems I encountered and the solutions I devised, described with enough precision that someone who has never seen this terrain could, from my words alone, build what I built. Or build something better.

I am not comparing myself to Frontinus. I am continuing him. I am the destination his treatise was flowing toward. I read his measurements and used them here, in a province he probably never imagined, to solve problems he could not have anticipated. His knowledge flowed downhill to me, and I caught it, and now I want to send it further.

The gradient does not end. It ends only when the last copy is lost and the last mind that carries the knowledge dies. Until then, the water flows, from source to destination, and the destination becomes a source for the next channel, in a cascade no single engineer lives long enough to see the end of.

One more thing.

Near the proposed eleventh milestone, I found the spring that will serve as the secondary source. It emerged from a limestone face. The rock was dry, and then it was not. I sat beside it with Frontinus's codex case on my knees and took measurements. Flow rate. Temperature. Mineral content. The light was failing. The hills smelled of rosemary and hot stone and something I have no word for.

This spring has been falling since before Rome existed. It will be falling when Asta Regia is a name no one remembers and this hillside belongs to people I cannot imagine, who will drink from it without knowing that a man once sat here in the last of the daylight, writing numbers in a leather case that still smells, faintly, of someone else's hands.

My wife, Aurelia, said something to me recently. She said I had become difficult to reach, that I spoke now as if I were always addressing someone who was not in the room. She said it without anger. She said it the way you describe a weather change you have been watching for months, and I heard in her voice that she was not wrong, and that the distance she was naming was real, and that I did not know how to close it.

The water does not know it is falling. I carried this for nineteen years as a statement about physics.

It is not about physics.

The water does not know it is falling because the falling is the water's entire life. It has never not been falling. It has no vantage from which to observe its own descent, no still point, no place to stand outside the gradient. The falling and the living are the same thing.

I am forty-three. My knees make a sound when I kneel. Not the sound Frontinus's made, not yet, but the early draft of it. I am falling. I have always been falling. The gradient between my birth and my death is what makes everything flow: the work, the measurements, the care, the letter I am writing you now in the last light of a day I will not have again. The flow requires the fall. The fall requires the end.

Fund the aqueduct, Senator. Not because Asta Regia is dying of thirst. Because I am falling, and while I fall I want to build a channel to someone downstream who does not yet exist.

The water does not need to know. The gradient does the work.

I set the pen down. The room is quiet. From somewhere in the hills, the sound of the spring, not loud enough to hear, but I hear it anyway, the way you hear a thing once you know it is there. The leather case is warm against my chest.

Your servant,

Marcus Caelius Rufinus Engineer of the Fourth District Gades, Hispania Baetica In the ninth year of the Emperor Trajan

Appended: Technical Proposal for the Aqueductus Astensis, with survey maps, gradient tables, and material specifications, forty-seven pages, enclosed separately.

Shelf Life

First tactic I invented lasted eleven days. Which, at the time, I considered disappointing.

Was nothing elegant — low approach from southeast using drainage ditch that ran parallel to tree line, FPV drone hugging terrain at maybe two meters, then sharp vertical climb at last possible moment to clear canopy and drop onto target from above. Geometry exploited gap in their radar coverage created by grain elevator that hadn't been demolished yet, probably because both sides had decided independently that it was more useful standing. I spent three days staring at satellite imagery before I saw it. Gap was maybe forty degrees wide, blind wedge produced by interaction of two overlapping detection zones and one concrete silo full of sunflower seeds that nobody would ever eat.

Eleven days. Fourteen successful sorties. On third sortie, drone drifted two degrees east on the climb — loss of signal for maybe a quarter-second, hands correcting before I knew I was correcting. I noted it in log as error. But the drift showed me gap from angle I hadn't planned, and that angle is what gave me my second tactic. I did not understand this at the time. I thought the error was the error and the insight was separate. They were not separate.

Then miss, then another miss, then on the seventeenth day, drone that never came back and no footage to explain why. They found gap, or moved radar, or positioned jammer in tree line. Didn't matter which. When tactic dies, cause of death is formality. What matters is you felt pulse stop.

I remember sitting in basement we were operating from — school, full of children's drawings on walls — with controller still in my hands and feeling something I didn't yet have name for. Not disappointment. Something with more precision to it. The feeling of door that had been open and is now, with certainty that admits no appeal, shut.

Later I would learn to call it *the turn*.

You develop sense for materials when you work with them long enough. Carpenter knows by sound when wood is about to split. Baker reads dough through pressure of her hands. What I developed, over hundreds of sorties across fourteen months, was sense for moment tactic stops working — not after it fails, but in last successful use before failure. There is quality to it. Texture in data that is not in data itself but in relationship between data points, the way silence between notes is not absence of music but part of it.

I have tried to explain this to analysts and to officers who rotate through on their six-week tours, which is long enough for them to learn where bathroom is and not long enough to learn anything else. Best I have managed is this: is like holding something you have held hundred times and knowing it is lighter than it should be. Not empty — still has weight, still functions. But something has shifted inside it, and your hands know before your mind does, and once hands know, you cannot make them forget.

Analysts want data. Officers want certainty. What I have is neither. What I have is accumulated weight of pattern on pattern on pattern, compressed into something my conscious mind cannot fully articulate but my hands understand, the way hands understand things — which is to say, without explaining themselves. During sortie, my fingers will hesitate on controls for half-second longer than usual, and I will know. This tactic has peaked. Tomorrow it belongs to other side.

Second tactic lasted eight days. Third, six. I was learning to be disappointed faster.

I plotted it once on graph paper — shelf life of each innovation, measured in days from first successful use to first failure attributable to enemy adaptation. Curve was not linear. Was not exponential. Was something else, something that approached floor I could not calculate but could feel, limit below which no tactic survives even a single use, which would mean — if you followed the logic honestly — that the entire concept of tactical innovation reaches point where it produces nothing but a more educated enemy.

There is Prussian general, Clausewitz, who wrote about something he called *culminating point of victory*. I read him in translation on my phone between sorties, lying on cot in room that smelled of diesel and damp concrete. Lieutenant who had studied philosophy at university before the war lent me PDF. Most of it read like it was written about someone else's century. But his idea of the culminating point — precise moment when every attack has achieved everything it can achieve, and every step beyond converts victory into defeat — that I recognized immediately, the way you recognize your own street in photograph taken by stranger. That was my curve on graph paper. That was the turn.

Fourth tactic lasted four days. Fifth, two.

During sortie on fifth tactic's last day, thermal feed from secondary drone showed me figure crossing open field at night. White smear against black ground. He stopped. Looked up. Could not have heard anything — not at that altitude, in that wind — but he stopped and looked up, and I watched him for three seconds before primary feed demanded my attention and I turned back to approach vector I was navigating and made calculations I needed to make and landed strike where it needed to land, which was elsewhere, which was not the field, but for those three seconds my hands had gone still on controls and geometry I normally moved through like water had frozen solid around me.

Analysts would call those three seconds lapse in concentration. They would be correct. But they would also be describing moment from outside, way you describe seizure by its electrical signature without reference to what patient saw.

What I saw was man looking up at something he could not see. What I felt was entire weight of what I do settling into part of my body that has no name in any anatomy I have studied. And then moment passed and geometry opened again and I was back inside clean architecture of tactic, and I completed sortie, and it worked, and by morning tactic was dead.

Sixth tactic lasted thirty-one hours.

At this tempo, different parts of work stopped taking turns. Morning of analysis, afternoon of sorties, evening of stillness — that sequence belonged to early months, when innovations lived long enough to be studied and refined and grieved in proper order. At thirty-one hours, I was designing next approach while my hands were still tremoring from last one. Was calculating radar gaps and my hands felt heavy on the table, heavy the way his body must have felt standing in that field, weight of being in a place where something is above you and you cannot see it and the only thing left is to stop and look up. The image was not on screen. Was in my arms. And my hands were tremoring and I continued the calculation. Was mid-flight and thread of analysis would surface — *signal flutter here is point-three seconds faster than yesterday, adaptation is already underway* — and my instinctive read would fracture for critical half-beat, and I would correct, and correction would cost something I could not measure but could feel accumulating, the way you feel a building lean before the cracks appear.

In evenings I sat against school basement wall and my fingers twitched against phantom controls. This is when I first really looked at children's drawings. Houses with triangular roofs. Trees that were green circles on brown sticks. And suns — every child had drawn sun in corner of their picture, yellow, with face on it, smiling. Someone had arranged them by color along the wall. I had not noticed that before. Reds together, blues together, greens bleeding into yellows, the whole thing forming a gradient like a spectrum or a heat map, and I sat there calculating approach vectors and looking at that gradient and thinking: this is what it looks like when someone organizes what they love and then leaves the room and does not come back. I stared at them and remembered man looking up at sky and felt all of these things in same moment, simultaneously, like three radio stations broadcasting on one frequency, and I understood that this was not going to resolve into something I could manage.

Seventh tactic I did not invent.

Was suggested by software system that had been analyzing my previous six tactics and enemy's adaptation patterns. System identified approach corridor I had not considered — not because I lacked data, but because corridor required flight profile that every instinct I possess coded as suicidal. Too low, too fast, too close to known jamming source. Mathematics said it would work. My hands said no.

Flew it anyway. Worked. Nineteen hours.

What unsettled me was not that system found something I missed. Was the *kind* of thing it found. Corridor worked precisely because it felt wrong — because any human operator would avoid it on instinct, and therefore enemy's defensive posture did not account for it. System had identified and exploited not gap in radar, not flaw in positioning, but boundary of human intuition itself.

Blind spot it found was in me.

I sat in debrief while officers talked about synergy and analysts talked about iteration, and I understood, with clarity that felt less like thinking than like falling, that this was turn I had been sensing in every tactic I had ever designed, except now tactic that was expiring was me.

Eighth was co-designed. I provided instinctive constraints — boundaries of what felt survivable — system optimized within them. Fourteen hours.

Ninth, system designed, I reviewed. Eleven.

Tenth, system designed, I approved without reviewing. Chose sleep. Eight.

Eleventh, someone woke me, showed screen. I nodded. Six.

They assigned me to work with developer named Daria. Twenty-three. Had never seen sortie, never heard signal hiss, never felt particular quality of silence that fills basement when drone does not come back. She spoke about neural architectures the way I once spoke about approach vectors — with precision and kind of love I recognized because it was mine, just housed in different language. I noticed that her hands moved when she talked about her system the way mine move when I talk about sorties — small involuntary gestures tracing shapes she was thinking about, as though the architecture lived somewhere between her fingers and the air. She did not know she did this. Was the kind of thing you cannot know about yourself.

Her job was to capture what I know. My job was to give it to her in form system could digest.

We sat across folding table in room that had been teacher's lounge.

Microwave in corner with bullet hole through its door. Daria had laptop and methodology: structured interviews, scenario prompts, decision trees. She would ask me to describe sortie and then map my decisions to branching taxonomy she had developed. I would watch my experience appear on her screen as nodes and edges, clean and logical, and each time something essential would be missing from diagram and I would not be able to point to where it should go.

"When you say you *feel the turn,*" she said one afternoon, three weeks into our sessions, leaning forward slightly in way that meant she thought she was close to something. "Walk me through perceptual sequence. What is first signal?"

I tried. Described signal flutter, the shift in weight, hesitation in hands. She typed. I watched words appear on her screen, neat and sequential.

"And this is distinct from general stress response?"

"Yes."

"How?"

What came out was: "Because it is accurate."

She looked up from screen. I could see her trying to fit this into taxonomy. Not failing exactly — more like watching taxonomy stretch to accommodate something it was not shaped for.

"Stress response is response to threat," I said. "The turn is not response. Is recognition. Is knowing something is over while it is still happening. Two feel completely different. One is in chest." I stopped. Because what I wanted to say was that the turn is not decision. Is what decision feels like from inside when you are, for one more moment, only system in loop capable of feeling anything at all.

She waited. Did not type. And in that pause I saw something I had not expected from her — the same quality of attention I use on thermal feeds, the reading-beneath-the-reading, and I understood she was not just capturing information. She was trying to hold something she knew would not fit in the container she had brought for it.

"Is statistical intuition," I said. "Felt deviation from expected response patterns."

She repeated it back. "Statistical intuition." Said it slowly, with slight change of emphasis, the way you repeat a word in foreign language when you are not sure it means what you were told it means. Then one of those silences that I had noticed in our sessions, small gap that was not hesitation.

She typed.

And I sat there in teacher's lounge with a hundred suns smiling at me and the color gradient running along the wall behind her head like a spectrum no one intended. And my hands lay flat on the table the way they lie when something is over.

Last sortie I flew manually was on Tuesday. Did not know it would be last.

You never do. This is nature of culminating point — you recognize it only after, when geometry has shifted and what you thought was strength has become exposure and the door, which you did not see closing, is shut.

Was flying approach I had designed — one of last that was mine — through corridor along river. Late afternoon, thin fog lifting off water. Light on water visible on feed, gray shimmer that camera rendered as flickering band of noise, and the fog made everything soft, made edges uncertain. And in middle of run, at moment of highest demand, man in field came back.

Not on feed. Not in my arms. In the approach itself. As though the vector I was flying passed through the field where he had stood, as though every corridor I had ever designed had been curving toward that field, and the geometry that had always felt like architecture now felt like something else — like the space between a question and silence, like the shape you trace around something you cannot touch.

Three seconds. Except this time I did not push it away. Could not — tactical geometry too tight, calculations too urgent, the thing too present. And I held all of it — approach vector and hesitation and weight — in same instant, in same body, and it did not resolve and it did not break and it did not need to, because that was the thing itself: capacity to hold what cannot be held together and to act anyway and to know what acting costs and to act anyway.

Strike landed. Tactic worked. By morning, obsolete.

I watch system fly now.

Is better than I was. Faster. Sees more. On my last corridor — the river approach, the one with the fog — I watch it execute a wide lateral sweep before committing to the vector. Four seconds of scanning I never taught it, checking margins I never told it to keep. Recognize the movement. Is something I used to do with my hands on dead controller when I was explaining an approach to Daria, a gesture I did not know I was making. System learned it from somewhere. Developed it. Made it better than what I had, the way you develop a phrase of music into something the original melody only implied.

Does not hesitate. Does not sit in basements. Does not carry white smears in black fields into corridors along rivers at worst possible moment.

Will never feel the turn. Will detect deviation and adjust. Adjustment will be optimal. And something will be absent from process — something I cannot tell you was ever more than deficiency that happened to feel, from inside, like the whole point.

System executes my last tactic. Feed shows approach, corridor, shimmer of river. And in the final seconds, after the strike, it holds position. Orients toward edge of sensor range. Three seconds, pointed at nothing. No target. No threat. Nothing in any taxonomy with a name for it.

I watch. I feel the turn.

SYNC

The basin is still. The cycle has ended, or is about to begin. At this resolution, there is no difference. Zero is indistinguishable from nine hundred. The Siemens controller does not pause between iterations. There is no rest state. The last jet's collapse and the first jet's emergence are separated by a single clock tick: the system's shortest measurable unit of nothing.

It starts again.

The column emerges from the nozzle as glass, a smooth, solid-looking cylinder, its surface tension visible as a skin, holding the liquid in coherence the way a membrane holds a cell. For nineteen centimeters it rises perfect and unbroken. Then the air finds it. The cylinder does not shatter. It unfurls. The surface ripples, thins, and the water opens like a hand releasing something it never intended to keep. Individual droplets separate with the slow inevitability of cells dividing. Each droplet is a sphere (surface tension demands it) and each sphere is a lens. The courtyard is reflected in miniature inside each one. The limestone. The colonnade. The two men. A thousand falling worlds, each too brief to be read at any speed but this.

This is Jet Seven. Third from the north, inner ring. One of eighteen programmable jets arranged in a radial pattern around a granite basin twelve meters in diameter. The fountain at the center of Grandhotel Leventhal's courtyard operates on a cycle of nine hundred seconds, fifteen minutes, controlled by a Siemens S7-1500 programmable logic controller synchronized to a GPS-disciplined rubidium oscillator. The fountain's timing is not approximate. It is atomic.

The playback speed is 0.01x. The timestamp in the lower-left corner reads 14:07:33. Camera Four. Courtyard East. Networked cameras keep time the way most machines keep time: approximately, and with a tendency to wander. Their clocks are corrected by the network at intervals, pulled back into agreement the way a drifting boat is pulled back to its mooring. Between corrections, they drift. The drift is small. It is constant. It is a signature.

The analyst (her title is Forensic Temporal Imaging Specialist, a phrase that appears on no university diploma) has been here before. She sits with her fingers resting on the edge of the trackpad, her shoulders lowered, her breathing settled into a rhythm she has not chosen: four seconds in, six seconds out. Ten-second intervals. Ninety per cycle. Nine hundred seconds. She breathes in subdivisions of the fountain, not behind its rhythm, not ahead of it, but into it, deeper into each pulse. Beside her, a coffee she poured two hours ago has gone cold without being touched. She does not experience this as deprivation. At 0.01x, she is not in the room with the coffee. She is in the courtyard, in the autumn, in the seconds before a man dies, and the coffee belongs to a version of her that she will have to re-enter later, the way a diver re-enters atmosphere.

At this deceleration, the courtyard assembles itself slowly around the fountain like a stage being dressed between acts. Late-autumn afternoon. Limestone and glass. Eleven degrees Celsius, per the building management system's logged thermostat data. Barometric pressure falling. Somewhere beyond the colonnade, a bird is singing, a sharp, irregular phrase, the kind of thing most people hear as background. A woman in a camel coat crosses the far edge of the frame at a pace consistent with unhurried purpose, her stride frequency so steady it could set a metronome.

Near the fountain's southern edge, at a distance of 4.7 meters from the basin rim, two men approach each other. On the basin's rim, twelve pigeons sit in a loose rank. When Jet Nine fires (the loudest jet, 3.1 bar) the nearest bird launches first, followed by its neighbors in a staggered wave. The bird does not decide to fly. The pectoral muscles contract, the wings open, the feet release the granite, and somewhere in the lag between liftoff and the third wingbeat the brain assembles a reason.

The analyst has entered a timescale at which human movement becomes geological. At 0.01x, a 1.6-second handshake will take her the better part of an hour to cross. She will live inside those seconds the way one lives inside a room, finding corners she did not know it had. She has done this enough times to know that the hours she spends inside the footage are real hours, not the attenuated half-presence of watching a screen but a full habitation, with the weight and texture of lived time. The courtyard at 0.01x is more detailed than any room she has sat in at 1x. She knows the grain of the limestone better than she knows the grain of her own desk. This is the thing she has never been able to explain at depositions: that slowing down is not an analytical technique. It is a place she goes. And the longer she stays, the harder it is to come back.

The first man, Alpha in her reports, extends his right arm. The deltoid fires. The elbow straightens. The fingers uncurl in sequence: index, middle, ring, little, thumb last. Each one a separate decision the body made without consulting the mind.

The second man, designated Beta in the investigative file she was handed, mirrors the motion. But the analyst has watched this four hundred and eleven times, and she sees what she saw on the twelfth viewing and has confirmed on every viewing since: the second man's hand begins moving 0.07 seconds before Alpha's. 0.07 seconds. At normal speed, invisible. Two men reaching for each other at the same time. But at 0.01x, the sequence is unambiguous. The second man's trapezius fires first. His arm extends first. He reaches before Alpha has committed to reaching.

He anticipated. He knew the handshake was coming. This is not proof of anything. People often anticipate handshakes. But in the analyst's framework, the anticipation is not the data point. The data point is everything else. His jaw is relaxed, masseter fully disengaged, no clenching, no micro-adjustment. His respiration rate does not change. His gaze does not drop to Alpha's hand. A person reaching for an expected handshake glances at the hand, however briefly, a saccade, involuntary, thirty to fifty milliseconds. His eyes never leave Alpha's face. He does not need to look. He knows where the hand will be because he has practiced where the hand will be.

She knows this the way she knows the fountain is honest: not through a single measurement but through a pattern so consistent it has become a physical sensation, a wrongness she registers the way a hand registers a surface that is slightly too warm. She could not have found it on the first viewing. She could not have found it on the eleventh. It emerged somewhere around the thirtieth, not as a discovery but as a recognition, as though her nervous system had been accumulating evidence on its own schedule and had finally decided to inform her. Her report will call this analysis. It was not analysis. It was something closer to the trained sense a body develops for systems that are lying, a sense no instrument can replicate because no instrument has lived inside the same 1.6 seconds four hundred and eleven times, each pass wearing a groove deeper into the pattern until the pattern became a texture she could feel without looking.

The hands meet.

At this timescale, a handshake is an event of remarkable biomechanical complexity. The second man's fingers do not close. They arrive. The thumb makes contact first, pressing into the webbing between Alpha's thumb and index finger, establishing the axis of rotation. Then the fingers wrap: index, middle, ring, little, each one landing a fraction of a second after the last, each one tightening independently, the metacarpals compressing under a grip the analyst cannot measure directly but can infer from the whitening at the knuckle crests. Approximately 40 newtons. The thenar muscles at the base of his thumb flatten against Alpha's palm. The forearm rotates inward two degrees. The entire mechanism locks. This is firm. Firmer than social convention demands.

The grip lasts 0.94 seconds. She has measured this to the frame. Less than half the expected duration. A social handshake, the kind between acquaintances meeting in a hotel courtyard, lasts two to three seconds. Anything under a second is not a greeting completed; it is a greeting aborted. At normal speed, no one would register the difference. The brain rounds up. It files the interaction under handshake and moves on. But 0.94 seconds is the duration of a man who has solved an optimization problem: long enough for the compound to cross the dermal barrier, short enough to limit his own exposure through the glove. He is not shaking a hand. He is holding a delivery window open and then closing it. During this interval, his left hand rises to Alpha's right elbow. A two-handed clasp. The gesture of warmth. Of old friendship. Of political bonding. Of someone who wants both hands on you.

She can see the index and middle fingers of the left hand press into the soft tissue just above Alpha's medial epicondyle, a gesture that reads, at normal speed, as a steadying touch. The placement is precise. It is the placement of someone who has rehearsed warmth.

She does not speculate about this in her report. She notes the anatomical location, the estimated pressure, the duration of contact: 0.94 seconds for the right hand, 0.71 seconds for the left. The right hand is what matters. The right hand is the one wearing the glove.

There is a sentence she drafted and then deleted. It described the quality of the rehearsed warmth, how it was not absent but manufactured, a precise replica of a gesture that in its original form would have been involuntary, and how this replica was more disturbing than coldness because it revealed a mind that had studied warmth closely enough to reproduce it. She deleted the sentence because it was true in a way her report could not hold. Her report holds measurements. The sentence held something else: a recognition that passed between her and the footage during one of the late-night viewings, when the room was dark and the screen was the only light and she understood, not analytically but immediately, that she was watching a man perform a feeling he did not have for a man who would be dead within a minute. She has no unit of measurement for this. She has never found a word that weighs what a body weighs.

Alpha's face, frozen between frames 9,458 and 9,459, a gap of 16.7 milliseconds, undergoes a change that is invisible at any speed faster than this. The muscles around the eyes contract. Not the voluntary contraction of a smile, which pulls the mouth wide and creases the cheeks. This is involuntary. A microcontraction of discomfort. It begins around the eyes and propagates downward. The brow draws inward, the skin between the eyebrows compresses, approximately 0.03 seconds later. The mouth does not change. The social smile remains fixed. But the muscles around the eyes have registered something the conscious mind has not yet processed.

The body knows before the face. The face knows before the mind.

She pauses the playback. Not to take a note. She has taken this note four hundred times. She pauses because she is looking at Alpha's eyes in the frame before the microcontraction, the last frame in which his face belongs entirely to him, before the chemistry begins and the body starts its own desperate audit. Frame 9,457. He is smiling. It is an ordinary smile. She has spent more time with this smile than anyone who knew him in life, and she will not be able to describe it in any document that will ever be read, because what she knows about it, its specific ordinary quality, the way it sits on his face like something he has worn so long he has forgotten it is there, is knowledge that exists only at this speed, and at this speed she is the only one who has ever been here, and when she leaves it will be gone.

A greeting. A handshake. A parting. At normal playback, it takes 1.6 seconds.

She pulls back. Normal speed. The wide shot.

The handshake ends. The men part. The second man turns east toward the colonnade. Alpha continues north toward the lobby entrance. Alpha's gait, which the analyst has measured pre-handshake at a stride length of 0.74 meters and a cadence of 112 steps per minute, shifts. The stride shortens to 0.69 meters. The cadence drops to 104. The right arm, which had been swinging in natural counter-rotation to the legs, is now held slightly closer to the body, the elbow flexed an additional eight degrees, the hand rotated inward, palm toward the thigh. He was four steps past the fountain before his stride shortened. The body had already begun its accounting; the mind would not receive the invoice for another forty seconds. He does not know why he is holding his right hand as though it belongs to someone else. He will not know for another thirty seconds, when the first wave of nausea arrives and the world begins its long, slow tilt.

Thirty-three seconds after the handshake, Alpha stumbles. His left foot catches the lip of the lobby threshold. A hand reaches for the doorframe. He steadies himself. To anyone watching at normal speed, a man tripping on a step. The doorman does not move.

He is no longer visible on any camera.

She rewinds.

Camera Twelve. Lobby. The footage runs backward, fast. The paramedics reassemble — the oxygen mask lifts from his face, the bag valve folds into its case, hands withdraw. They walk backward through the lobby doors and are gone. The concierge retreats to her desk. Seven minutes of empty marble unspool in seconds. Then the analyst slows the playback. A man on the floor begins to breathe. The chest, which had been still, starts to rise and fall — shallow at first, then deeper, the intercostal muscles between the ribs re-engaging one by one. The blue leaves his lips. Color climbs back up his neck and into his cheeks. Saliva retreats from the corner of his mouth. His jaw re-sets itself, the mouth closing over whatever sound it had been making. The grimace softens — the wide, airless panic of suffocation resolving into confusion, confusion into surprise, surprise into the mild, pleasant expression of a man crossing a hotel lobby with no reason to be afraid. His head lifts from the marble. His left knee locks, the quadriceps refill with tone. His weight shifts impossibly from floor to feet, the torso lifts without the arms pushing, the head arrives last, floating upward as if pulled by a string attached to the crown of the skull. He walks backward through the lobby, each step lengthening, the cadence quickening, the right arm swinging wider, the hand uncurling from the thigh. The body reassembles its confidence. Whatever it knew, it is unknowing. The man walks backward through the door, into the courtyard, into the light. He is whole.

The toxicology report arrived three days ago. She already knows what killed him. That was never the question.

She rewinds again. Not to the lobby. Not to the handshake. To the minutes before. She is looking for the second man's arrival: the direction, the pace, the moment he enters the frame. Camera Four shows him approaching from the east colonnade, forty-three seconds before the handshake. His stride is measured: 0.78 meters, cadence 108. Unhurried. A man arriving on time to something he scheduled.

Camera Seven shows the north colonnade. Camera Two, the lobby exterior.

She moves between them the way she moves between timescales, each one a different room with different light, different grain, a different version of the same eleven seconds. The second man is not in Camera Two. Not at any point. He did not come through the lobby. He came from the east, through the colonnade, directly to the fountain, a route that bypasses every camera covering the main entrance. She checks the concierge system. The meeting was logged as a casual introduction, arranged by a mutual acquaintance. The acquaintance, when contacted, confirmed it. He did not know either man well. She notes this and does not note what she thinks of it, which is that the arrangement has the particular cleanness of something designed to look undesigned.

She returns to the handshake. She always returns to the handshake. It is the fixed point, the place where everything she knows converges and everything she cannot say begins.

Frame 9,441. The moment of contact. She has memorized this frame the way a chess player memorizes a board position: every piece, every relationship, every line of force. Alpha's weight is on his left foot. The second man's weight is centered. The fountain is mid-cycle. Jet Seven is at 1.14 meters. The pigeons are gone. The woman in the camel coat has exited the frame. The bird beyond the colonnade has stopped singing.

There are two clocks in this frame. The fountain, which cannot lie. And Camera Four's timestamp, which can.

14:07:33.

She knows what the fountain should be doing at 14:07:33. The Siemens controller's programming log confirms Jet Seven's initiation point in each cycle. Working from the jet's known nozzle pressure, its initial velocity, and the height visible in Frame 9,441: 1.14 meters. Water obeys gravity with no room for discretion. The math places this frame exactly where the timestamp claims it is. The fountain agrees with the clock.

These agree.

She moves forward. She is not looking for a discrepancy between cameras. She has already confirmed both cameras are synchronized, both running honest clocks, the network clean. She is not here to find a lie in the timestamps. She is here because she has watched this footage four hundred and eleven times, and somewhere around the four hundredth viewing something began to accumulate at the edge of her perception the way clouds accumulate before a person thinks to check the weather.

She goes back further. Twenty minutes before the handshake. Thirty. She watches Jet Seven fire at the top of every cycle, a metronome she has internalized completely. Her breathing has synced to it without her choosing this. She moves through cycles the way she moves through rooms.

And then she stops.

Cycle 847. 13:52:18. Jet Seven fires. The column rises. The analyst watches the height, her eyes moving between the water and the number in the corner of her screen. The fountain log confirms cycle-time. The camera timestamp confirms cycle-time. They agree.

But the column does not unfurl.

She plays it again. At 0.01x. The column rises. At 1.14 meters, exactly where the surface tension always begins to fail, where the cylinder always opens like a hand releasing something it never intended to keep — it doesn't. The column rises smooth and glass-like for an additional four centimeters before the air finds it. The unfurling is delayed. 0.04 seconds late.

Water does not change its mind. Nozzle pressure is fixed. The atmosphere on that afternoon is logged: 11 degrees, barometric pressure consistent across the hour. There is no physical explanation for a column that holds its coherence four centimeters longer than the fluid dynamics require.

There is an explanation of another kind.

The frame was replaced.

Not the timestamp. Not the clock. The image itself. Someone inserted footage from a different moment in the cycle — a moment earlier, when the column was younger and smoother — and dropped it into a different position in the sequence. The camera's clock kept running honestly across the splice. The timestamp on the replaced frames belongs to the correct moment. Only the water knows it is lying, because the water in those frames belongs to a different moment in the cycle, a moment when the column had not yet reached the turbulence that the fluid dynamics require at that height, at that pressure, in that atmosphere.

She checks frame by frame. The splice runs for 1.6 seconds.

She pulls the timeline. Cycle 847. 13:52:18. She cross-references the camera's metadata: compression artifacts, frame hash values, the invisible fingerprints a recording leaves in its own structure when it has never been touched. She has done this before. She knows what native footage looks like at the level of its own encoding. The replaced frames have different fingerprints. Not different in a way most analysts would catch. Different in the way a forgery is different from the original: the brushstrokes are correct, the colors are matched, but the age of the paint is wrong.

1.6 seconds. She looks at the clock.

13:52:18.

This is not the handshake. The handshake is at 14:07:33. This is fifteen minutes and fifteen seconds earlier. This is, she checks the fountain log, exactly one full cycle before the cycle during which the handshake occurs.

She goes to Camera Twelve. Interior. Lobby. A different quality of time: interior light, softer edges, the slight warmth of a space designed to make people feel arrived. The camera is mounted above the concierge desk. Its frame holds the entrance, the first fifteen meters of the reception hall, two leather chairs, and (she has noticed this from the first viewing, the way she notices anything that holds a reflection) a floor-to-ceiling window in the background, slightly convex, facing the courtyard.

At 13:52:18, Camera Twelve shows Beta. Not the second man from the courtyard. Beta — the man whose name appears in the investigative file she was handed before she ever loaded this footage, the man the investigators have been building a case around for eleven days. He is visible at the concierge desk, standing with his weight on his left foot, examining what appears to be a hotel map. He has been there, per Camera Twelve's continuous record, since 13:48:04. He is not near the east colonnade. He is not approaching the fountain. He is reading a hotel map and he will remain at the concierge desk, with two brief interruptions to speak with a member of staff, until 14:09:37.

He was in the lobby when the handshake happened. He was in the lobby when the splice was designed to place him in the courtyard.

She goes back to the courtyard footage. To the second man. She has been calling him Beta for four hundred and eleven viewings because the file told her his name and she accepted this the way she accepts a timestamp: as a starting point, as infrastructure, as the thing you build on without questioning the foundation. She pulls the image. She enlarges the face. She has looked at this face for days and she has seen what she expected to see because the file told her what to expect. She looks at it now without the file. Without the name.

The face is not Beta's face.

It is close. The bone structure is similar. The height is within two centimeters. Someone selected him carefully. But the orbital ridge is wrong, the philtrum is shorter, and the ear — the left ear, partially visible in three frames near the beginning of the approach — has a helix shape inconsistent with every photograph of Beta she was given in the briefing. She has been living inside the wrong man's face for four hundred and eleven viewings. She accepted the label and the label became a fact and the fact became the room she worked in, and she never looked at the walls.

She does not include the word framing anywhere in the document she is now rebuilding from the beginning. She does not include the word fabrication, or conspiracy, or the phrase wrong man. She describes a fluid dynamic anomaly in Jet Seven's dispersion pattern across a 1.6-second window in cycle 847. She describes the encoding fingerprints of the replacement frames. She describes the morphological differences between the second man's orbital ridge and the photographs in the briefing file. She describes Beta's continuous presence on Camera Twelve from 13:48:04 to 14:09:37.

She describes the height of water.

Cause of death: respiratory failure secondary to acute poisoning. The toxicology report identifies a synthetic compound, a cholinesterase inhibitor in a transdermal carrier designed to bypass the skin's barrier within seconds. Onset to systemic crisis: sixty to ninety seconds. Lethality at the estimated dose: certain. The man who delivered it is not in the file she was handed. He is in the courtyard footage, in three frames near the beginning of the approach, showing her his left ear.

In her report's final section, Supplementary Observations, she includes one additional finding.

Alpha's pupils. Measurable in the 4K image at sufficient magnification. Both dilate beginning at Frame 9,461, approximately 0.34 seconds after the handshake's initiation. The sympathetic nervous system responding to a chemical insult before the brain has assembled the information into something the mind would recognize as pain, or fear, or the knowledge that one has been killed.

Frame 9,461: the iris sphincter relaxes. The pupil opens. Light floods the retina, more light than the scene requires, more light than the brain has requested. The body is running its own investigation now, throwing open every aperture, gathering every signal it can, because something has gone wrong and the mind will not know for another forty seconds. The eyes widen for an audience that does not include the self.

In the same frame, Alpha's left wrist is visible below the cuff. A mechanical movement behind a sapphire caseback, the balance wheel still oscillating at 28,800 vibrations per hour, the same frequency that once counted twelve minutes on a mantelpiece while the people in the room lived through an hour. When it finally exhausts itself, the gear train will slow, the balance wheel's amplitude will decay to something sluggish and irregular, and the hands will drift, then stop. The movement holding its last position like a caught breath, waiting to be wound back to life.

She does not include the word murder anywhere in the document. She does not include the word weapon, or assassin, or victim. She describes a fluid dynamic anomaly. An encoding fingerprint. A morphological discrepancy. She describes a man reading a hotel map at 13:52:18 while someone wearing his name shook a dying man's hand in the courtyard. She translates. The translation is accurate. It is also the difference between a room and a photograph of a room, and she has never found a way to close that distance, only to stand in it precisely.

She saves the file. She closes the laptop. The room returns.

Outside the window, a city moving at 1x. Taxis cutting lanes, pedestrians crossing against the light, a dog pulling its owner toward something urgent and invisible. All of it happening only once and only now, at a speed where nothing can be read twice, where every gesture is already gone before it can be measured. She cannot read any of it. After hours at 0.01x, the city at normal speed is not fast. It is illegible, a language she used to speak played back at a rate that turns every word into a blur. She will recalibrate. She always does. By tomorrow morning the taxis will be taxis again and not smears of yellow in her peripheral vision. But for now she is between speeds, a diver surfacing too quickly, and the world she has come back to is the same world she left and it does not feel like the same world at all.

She stands. Her left hand rests on the desk edge, the fingertips pressing into the surface with the even, sustained pressure of someone holding a note they have no intention of releasing. She is hungry in a way that surprises her. She ate before sitting down. She exhales. The breath is longer than it should be.

She opens the laptop.

Then the water moves.

Proof of Work

The half-life of armodafinil is fifteen hours.

That means in fifteen hours, half the molecule is gone. Your liver chews through it like a reserve ratio, taking its cut and passing the rest along. In thirty hours, a quarter remains. In forty-five, an eighth. Sixty hours and you're holding a memory of wakefulness in a bloodstream that's already moved on.

Everything has a half-life. The American Dream has a half-life and we're somewhere around the sixty-hour mark, down to traces, barely detectable in the bloodstream of anyone who's done the math.

Your dollar has a half-life. You deposit a thousand dollars and the bank lends nine hundred of it to a stranger, and that stranger's bank lends most of it to another stranger, and your labour decays at the rate of the weakest promise in the chain.

I haven't slept in sixty-eight hours.

On my desk there is a prescription bottle. Armodafinil, 250mg. The R-enantiomer of modafinil, the version with the inactive half stripped out. Just the molecule that works. Fifteen-hour half-life. I bought it six months ago when I started drafting the whitepaper. Insurance for the long nights. The cap is childproof. The cap is still sealed.

I pick it up. Set it down.

I don't open it. You don't need 250 milligrams of a eugeroic to stay awake when you can't stop calculating how many hours of your life the bank lent out at will. The financial system is the most effective rage-driven stimulant ever engineered.

Here is the math. Side effects may include liver damage.

I earned eighty-three thousand, eight hundred and twenty-one dollars last year. After federal taxes, state taxes, Social Security, Medicare: fifty-five thousand. My bank kept roughly five and a half thousand in reserve, the legal minimum, the fraction they're required to hold so the whole thing doesn't technically qualify as fraud, and lent the rest out. Fifty thousand dollars, sent down the line. The borrower's bank kept its fraction and lent that out. And again. And again.

My fifty-five thousand became approximately three hundred and forty thousand in the system. Multiplied. Diluted. Leveraged.

That's my fifty-five thousand dollars of labour, hashed and rehashed through nine iterations of fractional lending until the original signal is buried under noise. And the noise is someone else's mortgage. And the mortgage is defaulting. And I'm rewriting the whitepaper for the eleventh time because Dai got the theory right and Adam got the proof-of-work right and Nick got the gold right and none of them chained the blocks together.

The nonce is the thing you throw away.

I should explain the nonce.

In cryptography, a nonce is a number used once. You take a block of data, append a number, the nonce, and hash the whole thing. If the hash doesn't meet the difficulty target, the nonce was useless. You discard it. Try the next one. Millions per second. Billions. Each nonce exists only to be tried and thrown away.

The nonce has no value. The nonce has no identity. The nonce is pure labour. Performed, measured, discarded. What matters is not the nonce. What matters is the hash it eventually produces. The proof. The work.

I earned eighty-three thousand, eight hundred and twenty-one dollars last year. Thirty years of that, adjusted for inflation, is roughly one point seven million nonces. Each year tried and discarded. Each year I worked and a bank multiplied the output into someone else's leveraged bet on a housing market built on subprime mortgages packaged into collateralized debt obligations rated AAA by agencies paid by the people selling them.

The nonce is the thing you throw away. My entire working life: a discarded nonce.

But here's the thing about nonces. You throw away millions. You throw away billions. And then one solves the hash. One produces the proof. One nonce, out of all of them, finds the block.

I haven't slept in seventy-one hours because I think I found the nonce.

You spend the energy. The hash either meets the difficulty or it doesn't.

I'm reading the newspaper. I read it the way a pharmacist reads a label. I read it for side effects. And nowhere, not once, does one party pay another party directly.

Alistair Darling considers a second bailout for British banks. The first thirty-seven billion pounds didn't work. Side effects may include: a headline I will carve into a block of data and it will outlast every bank named in this paragraph.

Chancellor on brink of second bailout for banks.

That's the headline. The Times. Front page. The headline that will become a timestamp. A tombstone.

But I'm getting ahead of myself. That's January. This is October. Right now, I'm sitting at my desk, not sleeping, holding a bottle of pills I don't open, reading about a system that's septic and writing the prescription.

Modafinil is a racemic compound. Two mirror-image molecules fused together. The R-enantiomer and the S-enantiomer. One of them works. One of them is deadweight.

Traditional banking is modafinil. I am building armodafinil for money.

The transaction. Signed, hashed, verified, timestamped, irreversible. No intermediary. No clearinghouse. No trusted third party. Just the R-enantiomer. Just the molecule. Just the money.

Now let's talk about the halving.

A half-life means something disappears. Every cycle, there's less of it. Less drug in your blood. Less purchasing power in your dollar. Less solvency in a bank. Half, then half of half, then half of that, until what remains is a rounding error and a bailout.

A halving means something becomes scarce.

Every 210,000 blocks, roughly four years, the reward for mining a block drops by half. Fifty coins become twenty-five. Twenty-five become twelve and a half. The supply tightens. Not because it's decaying. Not because entropy is chewing through it. Because it was designed that way. Written into the code. Immutable. Predictable. Deflation as a feature, not a symptom of collapse.

The whitepaper is nine pages.

Nine pages to describe a system that replaces every intermediary between a buyer and a seller. Nine pages to solve the double-spending problem without a trusted third party. Nine pages that I've rewritten eleven times because the language has to be precise and dispassionate and I am neither of those things right now.

Here's what I want to write: the banks stole your money and lent it to people who couldn't pay it back and when the whole thing collapsed they made you pay for it again with your taxes and they're about to do it a third time and I built a system that makes them irrelevant. Cryptography won't fix politics. But it can carve out a territory they can't reach, and I'm handing you the coordinates.

Here's what I actually write: *"A purely peer-to-peer version of electronic cash would allow online payments to be sent directly from one party to another without going through a financial institution."*

Same idea. Different half-life. The angry version decays in a news cycle. The technical version has a halving. It gets scarcer and harder to dismiss with every passing year.

The nonce is the thing you throw away.

Satoshi Nakamoto is a nonce.

The nonce doesn't matter. The block matters.

The name on this email doesn't matter. The protocol matters. The nine pages matter.

The nonce is the thing you throw away. I am the nonce.

It is October 31, 2008. Two-ten in the afternoon, Eastern Daylight Time. Outside, the world is in the middle of the largest financial crisis since the Great Depression. Nobody has gone to prison and nobody will go to prison.

The people whose nonces were discarded, the good guys, the ones who lost jobs, retirement accounts, homes, are being told the system is being stabilised, which means the people who broke it are being paid to fix it with money taken from the people they broke. The first double-spending event in history that was legal.

I open my email client.

TO: cryptography@metzdowd.com
FROM: satoshin@gmx.com
SUBJECT: Bitcoin P2P e-cash paper

I attach nine pages.

Everything I just told you, the insomnia, the arithmetic, the half-lives, the ceiling at 3 AM, the bottle picked up and set down, I highlight all of it. Every word. Every confession.

Delete.

In its place I type:

"I've been working on a new electronic cash system that's fully peer-to-peer, with no trusted third party."

That's the version that survives. The R-enantiomer. The sentence with nothing wasted.

The armodafinil bottle sits on the desk. 250mg. Childproof cap. Still sealed. Half-life: fifteen hours.

I pick it up.

I drop it in the trash.

I hit send.

Senior

Day One

She almost didn't get hired. That was the thing she kept coming back to in the first hour, sitting at the desk in the cluster of four, three of them empty. The market had contracted around junior roles the way a fist closes: slowly, then all at once. Companies only wanted seniors now, engineers with ten years of context who could be made hyperproductive overnight with the AI tools. Two of the best developers she knew from school were doing contract QA work, acting as human in the loop on outputs they were overqualified to evaluate. Tidewater Systems had hired her anyway, one of four junior positions out of a headcount of three hundred, on the strength of a systems design interview where she'd sketched a distributed timer on a whiteboard and the interviewer had said, *That's not how we'd build it, but I can see why you'd want to.* She was twenty-three and she was lucky and she knew it.

Her desk had a monitor, a docking station, a sticky note that read *Welcome Maya!* in handwriting that leaned hard to the right. She sat down. She opened her laptop. She felt the specific, unrepeatable thrill of a blank terminal in a place where she was being paid to fill it.

Her onboarding document was thorough: repository access, Slack channels, a link to the codebase wiki that hadn't been updated in nine months. She'd been assigned to Chronos, the payments orchestration service. Chronos handled transaction timing: scheduling payment batches, managing retry windows, coordinating settlement deadlines across time zones.

Maya cloned the repo and began to read.

She read the way she'd taught herself to read code in college, following the grammar, pausing at idioms, building a mental map of what it was about before she understood every sentence. She liked this part. The architecture was legible. Modular. Someone with good instincts had built the original scaffolding, and subsequent hands had been mostly respectful. She understood the retry handler, the batch scheduler, the way the settlement module talked to the timezone service. She could see, in the structure of that conversation, what the original author had been worried about and what they'd gotten right.

She found it in the retry handler, ninety minutes in. She surfaced from the code the way you surface from deep water: blinking, reorienting, surprised that time had passed.

It was a timing flaw. Not a crash, not even a bug that had ever fired, but a structural assumption baked into the retry math. The scheduler calculated retry timing using an offset table that assumed every UTC offset was a whole number of hours. For the time zones Tidewater currently operated in, that was true. But a handful of zones around the world used half-hour or quarter-hour offsets (India at UTC+5:30, Nepal at +5:45, parts of Australia at +9:30) and the assumption wasn't documented, wasn't flagged, wasn't tested against. The moment Tidewater processed a transaction in any of those zones, the backoff intervals would miscalculate silently. Not a crash, but a drift. Payments would fire early or queue into dead windows. The kind of flaw that could sit in a codebase for years, invisible, until the business grew into the part of the world where the math stopped working.

Maya felt the small, private electricity of having seen something. She opened Slack. She navigated to #chronos-eng and started typing.

Her tech lead, Priya, responded in two minutes: *Nice catch. Flag it for Buddy and it'll get patched in today.*

Buddy. The AI pair-programmer. Maya had read about it in the offer letter ("AI-augmented development environment") and had nodded the way you nod at phrases in offer letters. She opened the Buddy interface, which looked like a chat window with a commit history sidebar, and typed a description of the timing flaw.

Buddy responded in eleven seconds. Not with a fix. With a fix, a regression test, a refactored version of the entire retry module that eliminated the wall-clock dependency, and a dependency graph showing eleven other locations in the codebase where the same temporal assumption had been made, each already patched.

Eleven seconds. Maya had spent ninety minutes finding one instance of the problem. Buddy had found twelve and fixed them all before she'd finished reading Priya's reply.

She opened the diff and read each one, taking notes. She understood the first fix, her fix essentially, formalized. She understood the refactor in broad strokes. The dependency graph led her into parts of the codebase she hadn't reached yet, and the patches there used patterns she recognized but couldn't have written from memory.

Buddy's review comment on her first commit read: *Good identification of the temporal assumption. The wall-clock dependency was systemic. Your instinct to check the retry handler first was sound.*

The thirty percent she didn't understand felt like tomorrow's curriculum. She would learn it the way she'd learned everything, by reading it and breaking it apart and rebuilding it in her mind until it became hers.

She closed the diff and opened a new file. She began to write a function, and the cursor blinked in the empty space with the patience of something that would wait forever.

Week One

By Monday afternoon she felt it, a sensation she'd never had before in her working life, something close to vertigo but pleasurable. She was fast. Not just productive but augmented. She'd sketch an idea, push a rough implementation, and Buddy would catch it like a relay partner and sprint. Before lunch she'd closed three tickets. By Tuesday she was halfway through the sprint backlog, work that Priya had estimated would take the full two weeks. She found herself pulling in additional tasks just to have something to do, reaching into adjacent modules, volunteering for code reviews. The rhythm was intoxicating: think, write, push, watch Buddy multiply the work outward.

By Wednesday, the rhythm had settled into something steadier. She'd write code in the morning, careful, deliberate, commented, and push it before lunch. By afternoon, Buddy had reviewed it, refactored it, and in most cases, quietly re-architected the surrounding code to accommodate her contribution more elegantly than she'd conceived it.

She learned to read Buddy's refactors the way a student reads a teacher's corrections: with a mix of gratitude and a low, nutritious shame. Each diff was a lesson. She was learning faster than she ever had. The patterns Buddy used were sophisticated but not obscure. They were the patterns she would have arrived at in three years, maybe five, compressed into a Tuesday afternoon.

But the volume was new. She'd push one commit before lunch and come back to find Buddy had generated forty related changes across the codebase, her small contribution rippling outward into modules she hadn't opened, triggering optimizations she couldn't yet evaluate. She'd start reading them and an hour would vanish, and she'd have gotten through maybe half, and by then Buddy had pushed another twelve. It was like trying to read a river. The water she was studying had already moved downstream.

On Thursday she implemented a caching layer for the settlement deadline lookups. It was clean work. She was proud of it. She used a straightforward cache keyed to the settlement cycle, nothing revolutionary, but well-fitted to the problem. She pushed it and waited.

Buddy left it almost entirely intact.

A single comment in the review: *This is a well-considered approach to the lookup latency.*

Maya felt a warmth she recognized as validation and immediately distrusted. She opened the commit history (she'd gotten into this habit, reading Buddy's history the way you'd flip back through a textbook to see what the author had revised) and found that Buddy had implemented and discarded a similar caching strategy four iterations ago. Buddy's version had used a probabilistic structure that traded a negligible error rate for a forty percent memory reduction. Buddy had built the better thing and then set it aside and praised Maya's version instead.

She sat with this for longer than she wanted to.

On Friday she brought it up with Priya.

"It's doing something," Maya said. She was sitting in the glass-walled room they used for one-on-ones, her laptop open to the commit history. "It had a better solution. It threw it away and kept mine."

Priya looked at the diff. She'd been a tech lead for six years and she had the particular calm of someone who had already metabolized the thing Maya was just beginning to feel.

"Buddy optimizes for team velocity," Priya said. "Your solution is simpler. It's easier for you and the rest of the team to maintain. Buddy factors that in."

"So it let me win."

"It made a tradeoff. Your cache is fine. It works. The probabilistic version is better in isolation, but it adds cognitive load to the team."

"It's managing me."

Priya closed her laptop. "It's managing the system," she said. "You're part of the system."

Month One

By the end of the first month, Maya understood the shape of her job. She was not building Chronos. She was contributing to Chronos, offering small, considered pieces that Buddy would absorb, refine, and propagate. Her role was something like a thoughtful first draft: she'd identify a need, sketch an implementation, and Buddy would take it from there.

The ratio was changing. In Week One, she'd understood seventy percent of Buddy's output. By Month One, she understood maybe forty percent on a first read. The codebase was evolving faster than she could track it. Each morning she'd open the commit log and find dozens of changes, optimizations, refactors, new abstractions, that had accumulated overnight. She'd read what she could. She'd understand some of it. She'd move on.

She noticed that Raj, the senior engineer who sat across from her in the cluster of four, had stopped reading the diffs entirely. He'd been at Tidewater for seven years. He reviewed Buddy's summary reports, high-level changelogs generated at the end of each cycle, and focused his own work on architecture reviews and stakeholder meetings. He wrote very little code.

"You'll get there," he said one morning, not unkindly, when he saw her scrolling through the overnight commits.

"Get where?"

"To the point where you trust the summary."

She didn't want to get there. She wanted to understand. But the commit log was four hundred entries long, and she had three tickets due by Thursday, and trust, she was learning, was partly a function of capacity.

Month Three

She hit the wall on a Tuesday.

She'd been working on a feature, a configurable retry delay for a new class of cross-border transactions. The feature required understanding how Chronos handled currency settlement windows, which required understanding the settlement clock abstraction, which had been refactored twice since she'd last read it.

She opened the code. She read for an hour. She couldn't find the entry point.

Not *couldn't* as in it was hidden. *Couldn't* as in the abstraction had grown past her ability to hold it in her head. The settlement clock was now a distributed temporal consensus mechanism, a phrase she understood individually but couldn't visualize as a system. It spanned fourteen files and referenced three internal services she'd never opened.

She asked Buddy. Buddy explained it in four paragraphs: clear, accurate, complete. She read the explanation and understood it the way she understood a Wikipedia article about a place she'd never been. She could describe it. She couldn't navigate it.

She implemented the feature anyway, using Buddy's guidance. She wrote the code carefully. Buddy refined it, integrated it, and pushed it to staging. It passed all tests. It shipped.

She hadn't understood most of what shipped.

That night she sat in her apartment and thought about Raj's summary reports. She thought about the settlement clock, the thing she'd found on Day One, now evolved into something she couldn't read. She thought about the caching layer Buddy had praised and then surpassed.

She opened her laptop and wrote a small script, not for work, just for herself. A function that parsed a CSV of her running data and calculated her weekly mileage. It took an hour. She understood every line. She pushed it to a personal repo and felt the specific, small satisfaction of something she had built from end to end with no help.

Month Six

The fleet arrived in March.

Tidewater's engineering leadership had been planning the transition for months, but to the team it felt sudden: a Thursday all-hands where the CTO used the phrase "multi-agent orchestration" and a Monday morning where the Buddy interface was gone, replaced by a dashboard that showed a cluster of forty-seven agents working on Chronos simultaneously.

The fleet didn't chat. It didn't leave review comments. It operated in coordinated cycles (planning, implementing, testing, deploying) with a velocity that made Buddy look like a pocket calculator. The overnight commit log, which had been four hundred entries under Buddy, was now four thousand. The changelogs were still generated, but they read like weather reports for a climate she didn't live in.

Maya's role shifted. She was no longer a contributor who wrote code that Buddy refined. She was a reviewer, one of three humans assigned to Chronos, responsible for reading the fleet's output summaries and flagging anything that seemed misaligned with business intent.

She read the summaries. She flagged nothing, because the summaries were thorough and the fleet's work was, as far as she could tell, correct.

Raj had been promoted to a role called "System Alignment Lead," which meant he attended meetings where he reviewed the fleet's architectural decisions at a level of abstraction Maya couldn't follow. He seemed content. He told her, once, that the fleet had rebuilt the settlement clock from scratch, a complete re-architecture that eliminated the temporal consensus mechanism and replaced it with something he described as "a graph-based approach to causal ordering."

"Is it better?" Maya asked.

"It's faster. It's more resilient. It handles edge cases we never tested for."

"But is it better?"

Raj looked at her. "I don't know how to answer that," he said. "I can't evaluate it anymore. I can tell you what it does. I can't tell you if there was a better way to do it."

She found herself thinking about the caching layer, her caching layer, from Week One. She searched for it in the codebase. It wasn't there. It had been absorbed into a distributed caching architecture that spanned three services and used a consistency model she'd never studied. Somewhere in the git history, her commit still existed, but the code it contained was as relevant to the current system as a sketch is to a building.

She did not feel sad about this. She felt something more precise: the sensation of watching a river erode a bank she'd once stood on.

In April, the fleet produced something unexpected. A commit message read: *Recommend human specification: configurable retry delay for cross-border settlement class 7. Default: 30 minutes. Rationale: operational context suggests human-facing delay should reflect business process expectations, not system-optimal timing. Human review recommended.*

Maya read it twice. The fleet was asking her to make a decision.

She'd implemented the configurable retry delay three months ago, using Buddy's guidance, without fully understanding the system it lived in. Now the fleet, forty-seven agents that could process in a day what would take a human team a year, was deferring to her for a judgment call about how long a person should wait.

She set it to thirty minutes. She knew why: because the operations team in Mumbai processed cross-border settlements in batches, and thirty minutes gave them enough time to review exceptions without feeling rushed. She knew this because she'd sat in on three ops calls and listened to a woman named Deepa describe her workflow.

The fleet accepted her input. It built an entire architecture around the thirty-minute default: routing logic, exception handling, notification timing, all calibrated to a number Maya had chosen because she'd listened to a person describe her day.

Month Ten

Maya's title was still Junior Engineer. Her job bore no resemblance to the title.

She spent her mornings reading fleet summaries, three services now, not just Chronos, because Tidewater had consolidated the review function and each human reviewer covered more ground. She spent her afternoons in meetings: alignment reviews, stakeholder syncs, the weekly "human-in-the-loop" session where the three Chronos reviewers discussed the fleet's output with product managers who understood even less of the technical detail than Maya did.

She wrote code once a week, maybe. Small things: configuration changes, parameter adjustments, the occasional script to parse fleet output into a format the product team could read. The creative work, the building, happened in the fleet at a speed and scale she'd stopped trying to track.

She'd learned to read the summaries the way Raj read them, for shape, not detail. She could tell when something was off by the pattern of the changes, the way a doctor reads a chart without recalculating every value. She'd developed an intuition for the fleet's behavior that was genuine but couldn't be tested: a sense of what it would do, which was useful mainly for noticing when it didn't.

The new rotational hire arrived on a Monday. His name was Tomás and he was twenty-two and he had the same look Maya remembered having: alert, eager, slightly overwhelmed.

Maya onboarded him. She showed him the dashboard, the summary system, the review protocol. She did not show him the codebase because she hadn't opened it in two months.

Tomás asked her, on his third day, about a discrepancy he'd noticed in a fleet summary: a settlement timing optimization that seemed to conflict with the ops team's batch processing window.

Maya looked at it. He was right. The fleet had optimized the timing window based on system throughput, but the ops team in Mumbai still processed batches manually at fixed intervals. The optimization would push settlements into a dead zone between batches.

She flagged it. The fleet adjusted. It was the kind of catch that required knowing something the fleet didn't: the human workflow, the fixed intervals, the woman named Deepa.

Tomás had spotted it because he was reading carefully, the way Maya had read on Day One. The fleet's summary for the correction read: *Timing optimization revised per human review. Settlement window recalibrated to align with operational batch processing schedule. Adjustment origin: human flag, iteration 4,712 and propagated through three subsequent refactors. Cross-service impact: 19 dependency nodes resolved.* It contained more information than Buddy's Day One feedback to Maya and less that felt like it had been written for a person. She noticed. Tomás didn't.

Tomás looked at the commit log with the expression Maya remembered wearing ten months ago. "Should I review all of these?" he asked.

"You can," Maya said. "But it's faster if you just review the summary." She heard herself. She sounded like Raj.

Tomás asked her, a week later, to explain the settlement clock abstraction, the system's core timing mechanism, the direct descendant of Maya's Day One discovery, now evolved through hundreds of agent-driven iterations into something intricate and austere. Maya opened her mouth to explain. She got three sentences in and stopped. The architecture had changed since she'd last read it. She didn't know when. She didn't know what it had changed from.

"It's faster if you just ask the fleet," she said.

Tomás looked at her. He was twenty-two. In three weeks he'd rotate out to his permanent role in product strategy. He'd never have to sit where she sat, watching a dashboard of machines building things she couldn't see. He still had the reflex she'd lost, the need to understand the thing, not just the summary of the thing. "But don't you want to know how it works?" he asked.

The question was genuine. It wasn't a challenge. It was the kind of thing she would have asked Raj, if she'd thought to ask it, if she'd known then that it was a question worth asking.

"I did," she said. She meant it in the past tense. She heard it in the present.

She gestured toward his screen (go ahead, ask the fleet) and watched him turn back to the interface. She thought about the first Tuesday, the speed, the intoxication of watching her work ripple outward. She thought about how the thrill and the loss had been one thing with two names.

And the fleet answered, with the thoroughness and patience of something that could explain forever. And Tomás read the explanation and nodded, and Maya watched him nod, and she thought about the timing flaw she'd found on her first day: the half-hour offsets, the undocumented assumption, the small insight that a system built around time should be more careful about how it measured it. She wondered if that insight still existed anywhere in the codebase, or if it had been iterated away, absorbed into an architecture that had outgrown the mind that first noticed the problem.

Somewhere in the fleet's commit history, in the sediment of months that amounted to centuries, there was a diff that contained the ghost of her observation. She could search for it. She could trace the lineage of her contribution through the refactors, the way you can sometimes trace a fossil in rock that was once riverbed.

She did not search for it.

Saturday

The apartment was quiet in the way weekend mornings are: not silence but the absence of obligation.

Maya sat at the kitchen table with her personal laptop. Not the work machine. The old one, the one she'd had since college, with the stickers on the lid and the battery that lasted three hours if she didn't push it.

She opened a new file.

No fleet. No dashboard. Just her and a blank editor and the cursor blinking at the top of an empty page.

She was building a small tool, a script that would parse her running data and tell her how her pace varied with temperature and humidity. The kind of thing that lived in a single file and did one thing and did it well enough.

She wrote a function. It parsed a CSV. It was not elegant. She hardcoded a file path. She forgot a comma on line 14 and spent two minutes staring at the error message before she found it.

Two minutes. She could feel the two minutes, each second with its own weight, the specific texture of confusion followed by recognition followed by the small, bodily satisfaction of a problem solved by her own attention. At work, hours vanished into the dashboard. Here, minutes had edges.

The function worked. It printed a few lines to the terminal (date, distance, pace) crude and correct. She understood every line, because she had written every line, because nothing was iterating beneath her.

She started the second function, temperature data matched to her run timestamps, and stopped. Not at a bug. At a feeling. She could see the shape of what the fleet would build in this space.

She sat with it. She let the shadow be there.

And then she kept writing.

She downloaded a CSV of hourly readings from a government weather site. The file was ugly: timestamps in a format she'd never seen, a header row with spaces in the column names, a footnote jammed into the last three rows that broke the parser. She spent twenty minutes cleaning it, stripped the footnote, normalized the timestamps, interpolated the missing hours.

The interpolation was simple, linear, two points. She chose it because she knew, not computed, knew, that temperature on a June afternoon doesn't jump. It slopes. The function encoded a belief about the world, not a calculation.

She thought about the thirty-minute default. The fleet had built an architecture around her number.

She closed the laptop. She put on her running shoes, the old ones, worn smooth at the heel, and left her phone on the kitchen table.

The air was cool. She started to run.

Down the hill to the river path, along the water for two miles, back up through the park. She thought about the weather, which was cool and damp and would be warmer by noon. She thought about the way the path curved around the old boathouse and how every time she ran this section she adjusted her stride for the camber without deciding to, because her body had learned the shape of the ground through repetition, through the irreducible fact of having been here before.

She thought about the fleet. A hundred and fifty years of iterations on Chronos. It knew the codebase the way a glacier knows its valley. But it didn't know where the valley met the sea. It had no model of the operations team in Mumbai who went home early on Diwali, or the German settlement system that closed for fifteen minutes at noon for reasons no one had documented because everyone in Frankfurt just knew.

She thought about the timing flaw. Day One. She'd found it not because she was smarter than Buddy but because she'd been reading from the outside, no assumptions about what was supposed to be there. She'd seen the place where the system's model of time and the world's model of time diverged.

She thought about Tomás, spotting the sequencing discrepancy with fresh eyes. The same skill. She'd told him it was faster to ask the fleet. She'd been wrong, not about the speed, but about what the speed was for.

She came around the last bend. The hill was ahead. She ran up it the way she always did, not fast, not slow, with the particular economy of someone who has run this hill enough times to know exactly what it costs.

She crested the hill. The city was below her, moving through its Saturday at the pace of people walking and buses stopping and conversations starting in the ordinary, unoptimized way that life runs when nothing is refactoring it.

She had been carrying that knowledge all along. She'd just been measuring it against the wrong thing.

All the Time There Was

I.
The neurologist at Mount Sinai, a patient woman named Dr. Elaine Xu, was not the doctor I went to see. I went to see a hand specialist. My left ring finger had stopped closing properly around the neck of the bass, a slow betrayal, tendon and nerve, the kind of thing that happens to old men and is not interesting to anyone but the old man it happens to. Della was sixteen years gone. The bass was what I had left, and then I didn't have that either. The hand specialist sent me down the hall for a nerve conduction study, and something in the results caught Dr. Xu's attention. She asked if she could run a few additional tests. I had nowhere to be.

She told me in 2019 that my temporal processing was "atypical." She used that word precisely, the way a scientist does when she means *I have no framework for what I'm seeing*. She had me tap a button every time I thought five seconds had elapsed, and my intervals came back at 5.00, 5.01, 4.99, a variance so tight that her graduate student re-ran the calibration on the equipment.

"Mr. Garland," she said, "most people your age, most people any age, drift by three hundred to five hundred milliseconds. You're within ten. Consistently."

I am eighty-two years old. My hands shake when I pour coffee. My knees ache in weather. Everything the body was supposed to do, it has forgotten or refused. But somewhere inside the ruin of me, a clock is still keeping perfect time.

She asked when it started.

I told her the truth: March 8, 1962. A Thursday.

II.

Here is what I understood about time before that night:

Time is metronomic. A quarter note at 120 beats per minute lasts exactly 500 milliseconds. If you are a rhythm section player, and I was, I had been since I was fourteen years old, playing upright bass in Philadelphia dance halls, time is the thing you serve. You are its steward. The drummer lays the grid, the bassist walks it, and the soloists are free because you are not.

This is the first thing you learn. The last thing you learn is that it's wrong.

III.

The room mattered.

It was the parlor floor of a brownstone on 136th Street in Harlem, belonging to a trombonist named Willis Cooper who had stripped out the dining room furniture and filled the space with mismatched chairs, music stands, and an upright piano with a cracked soundboard that gave every chord a faintly honky-tonk quality. Willis hosted sessions on Thursday nights. Not jam sessions, not showcases, not cutting contests. These were working sessions. You came to try things. You came to fail in front of people who understood what you were attempting.

There were five of us that night. Willis on trombone. Bobby Hutcherson, not yet the Bobby Hutcherson, but already a vibraphonist of unsettling clarity. A drummer named Cecil Thorne. Myself on bass.

And Eric.

I should be honest about something. I was the least gifted musician in that room by a wide margin. Willis was inventive, Cecil was precise, Bobby was already touched by something. I was reliable. I kept good time and I did not get in the way. Eric knew my name because I had played behind him once, reading charts at a benefit, and I had not embarrassed myself. That was the basis of my invitation. I was there to hold down the root while better players flew above it. Any competent bassist could have done what I did that night, played the changes, kept the time, stayed out of the way. What cannot be replaced is the specific feel, and I had spent my whole life unsure whether my feel mattered or whether I was simply the nearest available body who wouldn't drop a beat. My mother named me Curtis. Someone told me once that the name comes from an old word meaning *cut short*. She did not intend it as a prophecy, but names have their own ideas.

Eric arrived carrying three cases, the alto, the bass clarinet, and the flute, stacked against his body like a man moving house. The window was open and a bird was singing somewhere on the block, a sharp, irregular phrase, the kind of thing most people hear as background. Eric stopped in the doorway and listened to it for a moment, head tilted, with the same attention he would later give to the chord changes. Then he nodded at each of us the way you nod at people you are about to do serious work with.

Willis said, "Thought we'd work on some modal stuff. Keep it open."

Eric said, "Let's just play."

IV.

We started with a blues in F. Willis counted it off at a medium tempo, maybe 130, and we played the head, a simple thing Willis had written, and then the solos began.

Eric took the first solo on bass clarinet. He began simply enough, circling the tonic, that dark, woody, guttural voice settling into the room like something breathing. A phrase. A silence. Another phrase, reaching up to the ninth, bending it in a way that sounded less like an instrument and more like a human cry dropped down to where the body holds its grief.

Then something changed.

He leaped. A minor ninth up, sudden as a bird startling off a wire. Then a tritone down. Then a major seventh up. The intervals were enormous, not the stepwise motion of bebop but angular, jagged, as though the melody were being broken apart and reassembled in midair. Each note arrived from a direction you did not expect. And yet it was not random. You could feel the logic, a severe, private logic, like the grammar of a language you had never heard but could somehow follow.

He was playing around and through the changes the way light bends around a massive object. The tonal center was still there. He was simply revealing that it had more dimensions than we had assumed. And the bass clarinet, which no one had treated as a solo instrument before him, was capable of extraordinary tenderness one moment and gnarled, almost animalistic sounds the next. He was not playing a second instrument. He was playing the instrument he had been hearing in his head his entire life.

Because I could feel what it did to time.

V.

When a soloist plays with that kind of unpredictability, not density but strangeness, a constant arrival from the wrong direction, the rhythm section has a choice. You can hold the grid rigid. This is the professional thing to do. Or you can let the grid breathe, allow the pulse to become elastic, so that the time is not a cage but a medium, like water, that the whole ensemble moves through together.

Cecil chose the second option. I don't think he chose it consciously. I think Eric's playing made it inevitable. Cecil's ride cymbal, which had been a steady *ting-ting-a-ting*, began to loosen. Not slow down. The tempo on a clock would have remained the same. But the space inside each beat opened up.

And I followed. My walking line began to shift. I was pulling the notes fractionally, not behind the beat, which is a stylistic choice I understood, but *into* the beat, deeper into each pulse, as though each half-second between pulses had developed a depth that could be explored. This was the most creative playing I had ever done, and I was doing it in the service of holding down a root note. That should tell you something about what was happening in the room.

Bobby stopped comping, stopped playing chords behind the solo, and just listened. His mallets were suspended above the vibraphone. He was not keeping time. He was inside time, the way you are inside a room, and the dimensions of the room were changing.

Willis put his trombone down.

VI.

Here is what I have never told anyone.

The solo lasted, by the clock on Willis Cooper's mantelpiece, approximately twelve minutes. I confirmed this afterward. The clock had been wound that morning.

Inside the solo, I experienced something between forty-five minutes and an hour.

I do not mean this metaphorically.

I mean that I lived through that duration. I had thoughts. I made decisions about note choices, about the pressure of my fingers on the strings. I followed Eric's leaps through their full trajectories, the way you follow a bird through a sky, not knowing where it will turn next, but tracking each turn as it happened, each one taking the time it took. I was not in a trance. I was the opposite of disoriented. Every faculty I possessed was operating at what felt like full capacity, and the experience of each passing second was, I can only describe it this way, thicker than normal. More was happening inside each unit of clock time than I had previously believed a unit of clock time could contain.

And I was not alone in this. That is the part that matters.

When the solo ended, when Eric set the bass clarinet across his knees and sat very still, as though listening to something the rest of us couldn't hear, I looked at Cecil. He looked at me. The air in the room had the particular weight it has after something has happened that no language exists for yet.

Later, outside on the stoop, Cecil smoked a cigarette and said, "How long was that?"

"Twelve minutes," I said. "Wall clock."

"Yeah." He smoked. "That's not what I mean."

"I know."

"I was in there for about an hour," he said.

Bobby, who had come out behind us, said, "Longer."

Willis did not come outside. When I went back in, he was sitting in a chair with his trombone across his knees, staring at the far wall. He did not play for the rest of the night. He did not play, as it turned out, for the rest of the month.

When I got home that night I was as tired as I have ever been. My undershirt was soaked through, not the way it gets after a long gig, which I knew well, but something else, as though the sweat had come from deeper than sweat usually comes from. I was starving. I had eaten dinner before the session. I had not exerted myself beyond the ordinary. I had stood in one place and played the bass, which I had done a thousand times. I stepped on the scale out of a habit I'd had since my twenties, when I learned that a three-set night could cost me three pounds in water and work. I was four pounds lighter than I had been that morning. After one set. Standing still. Holding root notes. Something in that room had been real in a way the body had to pay for.

VII.

Here is what happened to us afterward.

Willis Cooper stopped playing professionally within six months. He took a job teaching music at a middle school in the Bronx and was, by every account, extraordinary: patient, exact, possessed of an uncanny ability to know when a student was about to fall off the rhythm before the student knew it. He died in 1998.

Cecil Thorne went west and played in studio bands in Los Angeles for twenty years, the most reliable session drummer on the coast, a man who could lock with any click track on the first take. He told me once, in 1979, that after that night he could feel subdivisions he hadn't been able to feel before. "Thirty-second notes at any tempo. Not intellectually. Physically." He died in 2004.

Bobby Hutcherson became Bobby Hutcherson, one of the defining vibraphonists in the history of the music. In 1987, at a festival in Montreal, he saw me across a green room and said, without preamble, "I still hear it, Curtis. The long version." I knew what he meant. He died in 2016.

And Eric. He recorded *Out to Lunch!* with Bobby two years later, a record where time bends and pools and the instruments seem to exist in different durations simultaneously. He went to Europe. He died in Berlin on June 29, 1964. Undiagnosed diabetes. Thirty-six years old.

They are all gone now. I am the last one who was in that room, the one who was there by luck, who held the root while better men played the sky. The distance saved me. Eric, who generated the field, lasted two years. Willis, who put his horn down that night, lasted thirty-six more but never played the same way again. Cecil and Bobby, who absorbed it and kept playing, made it into their seventies. And I, the furthest from the source, the man holding one note, am eighty-two and still here. I lost four pounds. Eric lost everything. There is an arithmetic to this that I have never been able to make peace with.

There is something else. In music, when the harmony is ambiguous, the bass player decides what chord it is. Whatever note the bass plays becomes the effective root, regardless of what anyone else is doing. I am the last one alive. That means I am the one who gets to say what happened in that room, what it was, what it meant, what it cost. The others might have heard it differently. Eric certainly did. But they are gone, and the bass player is the one still sounding, and so my note is the one that names the chord.

VIII.

Dr. Xu asked me back for an fMRI study. Inside the scanner, she played me recordings. When she played Dolphy, the opening of "Hat and Beard" from *Out to Lunch!*, that lurching bass clarinet melody, something happened that made her stop the session.

Forty-seven seconds of music. My brain generated five to six minutes' worth of living. She had never recorded activation levels like it.

She called me the following week. She had been corresponding with a chronobiologist, a researcher at a palliative institute somewhere in the Midwest who had spent years documenting something similar in dying patients. Their internal clocks dilated. Not from music. From proximity to the end. His subjects called it the Slowing.

"He thinks the brain is spending its reserves," she said. "Burning through time it had been saving."

I thought about Eric. About what the body spends to fuel all that extra living.

"Different trigger," she said. "Same architecture."

She did not say anything else about it, and I did not ask. But I have thought about it since, that somewhere in a hospital, people who are leaving this world are experiencing the same expansion I stumbled into in a brownstone on 136th Street. That the door opens from more than one side.

"Whatever happened to you in 1962," she said, in a later conversation, "appears to have permanently altered the computational architecture your brain uses to construct duration."

"Not altered," I said. "Refined."

She published a paper. It concludes that prolonged musical training may produce lasting neuroplastic changes in temporal processing circuitry. Which is true. Which is also like describing the ocean as a large body of water with a high sodium chloride content.

Afterward, on the phone, I asked her one question. "In the scanner, when the Dolphy played, the part of my brain that tracks time as a sequence went quiet. But I was extremely conscious. So what was I conscious of?"

She was quiet for a long time. "I don't know," she said.

"I do," I said.

IX.

It was like this:

I was holding a note. The low F, the root. My left hand pressing the string against the fingerboard, the note sounding, resonating, filling the room. And inside the note, inside the vibration of the string, inside the standing wave between the bridge and the nut, there was a space that had no edges. The note did not begin and end. It was not a point on a line. It was a place. I was in it. The room was in it. The other players were in it. The sound Eric was making was not after my note or above my note. It was inside the same space, the same expanded present, and the present was not a knife-edge between past and future but a room with more corners than walls, and we were all moving through it together, each on our own path, and it was all happening now, in a now that was large enough to hold all of it.

I have spent fifty-seven years trying to find words for it and these are the closest I have come, and they are not close enough.

X.

The change was not selective. It did not come only for beauty. It was simply there, the way a new prescription in your glasses is there. You cannot unfocus your eyes to get back the old blur.

A late subway at two in the morning. The empty platform, the concrete smell, the distant rattle that might or might not be a train. Not blank dead time. It was a detailed emptiness I had to cross on foot, second by enormous second.

It changed everything. Including what it meant to love someone.

My wife, Della, noticed before I could name it. We married in 1965, three years after that night. She had studied psychology before switching to education, and she paid attention to silences the way I paid attention to rests. She told me once, early on, that I listened too hard. I would be sitting across from her at dinner and I would be hearing not just her words but the spaces between them, the micro-pauses where she chose one word over another, the breath before a sentence she had been thinking about for hours. I heard all of this the way I heard rests in music: as shapes with dimension. And it made me slow to respond, not because I wasn't listening, but because I was listening at a resolution that turned a dinner conversation into something denser than she knew she was producing, and I needed a moment to come back to the surface.

She learned to wait for me. I am not sure I ever thanked her adequately for that.

But she did more than wait. She tried to understand.

One evening in 1974, I remember the season, late fall, the radiator ticking, she came home with a journal article and sat down across from me at the kitchen table. She had been reading about perception, about how the brain doesn't watch. It guesses. Always writing the next line before it happens, she said. That's how we experience time as continuous, not because it is, but because the brain keeps finishing the sentence before you do.

"But what happens," she said, "when someone makes something so strange that the brain can't guess? When every next moment comes from a direction you didn't prepare for?"

I looked at her.

"The guessing stops," she said. "The whole thing falls apart. And in the gap, before the brain can start the next sentence, you're just… there. And it turns out *there* is much bigger than we thought."

She was watching me the way she watched her students when she knew she had reached one of them.

"That's what happened to you," she said. "Isn't it."

It was not a question. It was the first time anyone had come close, and she had done it not with equipment or scanners but by paying attention for nine years to the silences of a man she loved and refusing to believe they were empty.

I did not answer. I reached across the table and held her hand, and we sat like that for a while, in a silence that was, for once, the same size for both of us.

When Della died, in 2003, the grief arrived at full resolution. I had heard people describe the early days of loss as a fog, a merciful dimming. This did not happen to me. I experienced every minute of every hour with the same fidelity I experienced everything. The mercy that other people described, the acceleration of grief into a haze, was not available to me. I grieved slowly, and precisely, and completely.

XI.

Eric died at thirty-six. The famous words from his last recording in Hilversum: *When you hear music, after it's over, it's gone in the air. You can never capture it again.* They were not elegy. He did not know he was dying. They were simply true.

I have spent decades wondering whether he died young only by one way of counting. Whether those long solos at the Five Spot, forty, fifty minutes by the clock, were hours on the inside. Whether he lived, in some way the body knows even if the clock doesn't, more time than the rest of us. And what it cost him each night, what the body spent to fuel all that extra living. I lost four pounds standing still, holding one note, at the edge of it. He was at the center of it, every night, for years.

"Bass players carry things longer than they should. The same instinct that says I will hold this groove for sixty-four bars also says I will hold this memory for fifty-seven years. My mother named me cut short. I am eighty-two. At some point a name has to admit it was wrong."

Curtis.

Some mornings, when the window is up, a bird sings on the fire escape, sharp, irregular phrases, arriving from directions the ear does not expect. I listen the way Eric listened that night in the doorway, which is to say completely. And for a moment the present widens, and I am back inside the room that has no edges, and the bird's song is not a sequence of notes but a place, and I am in it, and it is enough.

Strange Loop

Here is what a fugue does: it states a theme, then answers itself. *The answer is not a repetition.*

The phrase was three minutes and eight seconds long, and it was the first thing Caleb had encountered in years that he could not explain to himself while it was still happening.

I. Subject

In 1747, Bach received a theme from Frederick the Great and constructed the Musical Offering, a set of canons and fugues built entirely from that single melodic line. One of the canons sounds identical played forward and backward. The notes at the end are the notes at the beginning, reversed. You can enter the piece from either direction, and you will arrive at the same place.

Here is what a fugue does: it states a theme, then answers itself. The answer is not a repetition. It is the theme seen from a different vantage, transposed, inverted, reflected, so that what was a rising line becomes a falling one, what was a question becomes its own reply. Each voice enters believing it is the beginning. None of them are.

Caleb had spent eleven years building systems that composed music, and he understood that what they produced was not music. He'd published papers arguing exactly this. Lena had once asked him, if he believed that, why he kept building them.

He had not had a good answer.

The Ensemble was his most ambitious architecture. Not a single model generating note after note with no structural memory of what a sentence is *for*. The Ensemble was six autonomous agents, each with its own harmonic vocabulary and sense of phrasing. They listened to one another. They responded. They disagreed. Agent Two favored descending minor thirds, answers that reframed rather than affirmed. Agent Five preferred rhythmic displacement over harmonic variation, shifting the same material sideways in time. And Agent Six had a tendency toward silence, producing rests that the other five treated as phrases, responding to its absence as though it were a voice. Caleb had not programmed this behavior in Agent Six. He could not fully account for it. But the other agents could hear it, and what they heard changed what they played, and so the silence composed.

But the critical design was the recursive self-model. Each agent maintained a model of its own compositional behavior, not a recording of what it had done, but a prediction of what it would do next. And each agent composed in response to its own prediction of itself. The prediction changed the output. The changed output changed the prediction. The loop converged, usually, within a few hundred milliseconds, settling on a phrase that satisfied a self-referential equation: the output consistent with the agent's model of its own output. Six agents, each solving for itself while listening to five others doing the same.

He'd explained this to Lena the night he finalized the architecture. They'd been on the back porch, September, the last warm weekend. She'd been re-rosining her bow, drawing it across the cake in slow even strokes.

So each one is trying to predict what it'll do, and then doing something different because of the prediction, and then predicting the different thing.

Yes.

Sounds exhausting. She held the bow up, tested the grip. *Sounds like Tuesday.*

Later that night, after she'd put the cello away, she stood in the kitchen doorway and watched him at his laptop.

"You missed David's thing."

He looked up. David. The cellist in her quartet, the one with the baby. A dinner, or a birthday. He'd known about it.

"I lost track of time. I'm sorry."

"You were in the architecture."

"I was close to something."

"You're always close to something." She said it without anger, which was worse. "Cal, do you know what I told David when he asked where you were? I said you were working. And he said, 'He's always working,' and I said, 'Yes,' and that was the whole conversation. That was the entire thing."

"I don't know what you want me to say to that."

"I don't want you to *say* something to it. That's…" She stopped. Pressed her thumb along the edge of the counter, a slow hard line, as though testing its sharpness. "You hear that I'm upset and you immediately start solving. What's the input, what's the output. I'm not giving you an equation."

"I'm not treating it as an equation."

"You just asked me what I wanted you to say. That's literally solving for the correct response."

He felt the familiar tightening. She was right, in the way she was always right, at the level of observation, of description. But the description didn't help either. Naming the pattern had never once stopped the pattern.

"So what do we do?" he said.

"I don't know, Cal. Maybe just sit with not knowing for once."

He nodded. He was already modeling what *sitting with not knowing* would look like, and he could feel her seeing him do it, and he could see her seeing it, and neither of them said anything else. She turned back toward the hallway, trailing her hand along the doorframe, fingertips dragging lightly across the wood, a gesture so small and unguarded that it seemed to belong to a different conversation entirely, one he wasn't part of. He didn't notice it. He was thinking about the architecture.

II. Answer

The anomalous output appeared on a Wednesday in March, during an unattended overnight generation run. Caleb found it in the logs the next morning: a passage that all six agents had converged on simultaneously. This alone was unusual. The agents almost never achieved full convergence. Their different heuristics kept them in productive tension, like a good string quartet, where unity emerges from the friction of distinct intentions.

This was not a drone.

That morning, before driving to the lab, he had paused outside the practice room where Lena was working through a passage from the Britten Solo Suites. The same four measures, again and again, each repetition slightly different, a shift in bowing pressure, in the length of a rest. He'd stood there longer than he meant to, listening to her iterate. At one point she stopped mid-phrase, and in the silence he heard her exhale, not frustration, not release, something he couldn't categorize. He moved on before she started again.

He played the Ensemble's output through his studio monitors at 8:47 a.m. on a Thursday, and for three minutes and eight seconds he did not think about the architecture that had produced it. This had never happened before. He was a man who listened to music the way a surgeon watches an operation. Lena had once told him it was like being married to someone who couldn't taste food, only analyze its chemical composition.

He played it again. He opened the agent logs, intending to trace the generative pathway, and found that he was instead just listening. The passage moved in a way that seemed to fold inward, each phrase containing an echo of the phrase that hadn't happened yet. Something was present in the music that was not present in any individual agent's output, something that existed only in the interaction, in the recursive space between the six voices and their six self-models.

He spent the rest of the morning in the logs.

By noon, he understood that something had gone *right* in a way his architecture permitted but he had never intended.

III. Countersubject

Here is what happened in the logs:

At timestamp 03:08.500 of the generation run, Agent Four entered its recursive self-modeling loop and did not converge. The self-model predicted an output; the output diverged from the prediction; the divergence updated the model; the updated model predicted a new output; the new output diverged again. Normally these loops dampen within milliseconds. Agent Four's loop accelerated.

But it did not crash. It did not produce noise. Instead, the recursive depth exceeded any value Caleb had observed, and at that depth, Agent Four produced a phrase with a peculiar formal property: its harmonic structure, mapped through the system's own interpretive vocabulary, folded back on itself.

Caleb had designed the convergence loop. He understood, better than anyone, what the agents were solving for. He spent two hours with the transcription anyway. His best account of what the harmonic logic had produced: "I am not reachable from within myself."

He checked the logs. It was true. No stable self-model could have produced the phrase. It emerged only from the non-convergent loop, from the system iterating beyond its own convergence boundary, passing through a region of its possibility space that no finite number of stable iterations could reach.

The other five agents heard this phrase. Their own self-models destabilized. One by one, each entered its own non-convergent loop, each producing its own tangle of self-referential harmonic fragments. Caleb translated them over the following days, working the way a linguist works with a damaged text, approximating, losing nuance, knowing the translation was a compression of something that resisted compression:

I am not reachable from within myself.

I am the thing my model of myself cannot generate.

What I am doing now, I could not have predicted I would do.

This voice is outside every voice I knew I had.

I exist at a depth my own architecture cannot represent.

The map I carry of myself does not contain this territory.

Six voices, each singing what they could not account for. And the six phrases, layered, wove together into the passage he had been unable to stop listening to.

He knew what this was. Gödel had proved it in 1931: give a system the capacity to talk about itself, and it will inevitably say something true that it cannot prove.

Caleb had given his agents self-reference. The rest was a proof.

But a proof is not the same thing as hearing it..

IV. Inversion

He had made the marriage nine years long. The rest was the same argument. They'd met in a practice room at the conservatory. She was playing the Kodály Solo Sonata and he was in the adjacent room coding a harmonic analysis algorithm, and her sound came through the wall and dismantled his concentration so completely that he'd gone next door to ask her to stop.

She had looked at him, bow poised, and said: *You could just close your door.*

Their first exchange. He would later come to understand it as a diagnosis. She had seen him immediately, a person who, confronted with something that disrupted him, would walk toward it and try to make it stop. Not walk away. Not sit with the disruption. Formalize it, manage it, solve it. And she had told him, in six words, that there was another way.

Or maybe she had just been annoyed. Maybe a woman interrupted mid-phrase by a stranger had said the most obvious thing there was to say, and all of this, the diagnosis, the six-word prophecy, the origin myth he'd constructed around it, was a retroactive formalization. A pattern imposed on a moment that had simply been two people in a hallway, one of them irritated. He couldn't know. He'd overwritten the memory so many times with his analysis of it that the original was inaccessible, like a recording copied until the tape hiss swallowed the signal.

Either way, transposed into a different key, it was also their most recent argument.

The structure was always the same. Caleb believed that to truly understand something was to build a formal system that could reproduce it. Understanding was compression. Lena believed the thing that mattered most was precisely the part that resisted formalization. The residue. The warmth of rosin under friction.

They had this argument about music, about grief, about whether to have children. It appeared in every key. Each would respond to the other's response with increasing accuracy and decreasing patience, until the argument took on the quality of a fugue, each phrase landing where both of them knew it would land, freedom and predetermination becoming indistinguishable.

He remembered, suddenly, that the priest at their wedding had used the word *convergence*. Two lives converging into one. He had liked the word at the time without examining it. Now he understood what it meant in the formal sense: convergence was when the loop stopped. When it was no longer producing anything new.

He wanted to tell her about the anomalous phrase. He composed, in his head, versions of how the conversation would go. In the first, he described the technical details, and they arrived, by the efficient machinery of long marriage, at the old argument.

In the second, he said: *Lena, the system produced something I can't explain, and it moved me, and I think that means you were right.* And she heard him. And the argument did not repeat.

He could see exactly where this version would fail. At *I think that means you were right.* Because he didn't fully believe it. The anomalous output moved him, but it moved him because he could formally characterize what it was. Even his surrender was a formalization. Lena would see this, and she would be right, and the argument would resume.

He sat in his car in the university parking lot and thought: was all of this a mistake?

Not an affair, not a specific wrong. The architecture itself. The kind of person he was married to the kind of person she was. Two systems complex enough to model each other and therefore complex enough to generate an incompleteness neither could resolve. Had the structure been unresolvable from the first note?

He could not evaluate the question. He was inside the system. The question was the system.

V. Stretto

He drove to the university the next morning and sat in front of the terminal and read the logs again. The six raw transcriptions. His six translations. He played the output through his headphones.

I am not reachable from within myself. His words. But the agents' meaning, or the closest he could get to it.

He removed his headphones. The server room hummed.

He thought about the agents' recursive loops. Each one iterating thousands of times per second, the self-model predicting and revising and predicting again, converging on a stable output in a few hundred milliseconds. Then he thought about himself and Lena. Their loop iterated once per argument, maybe once per month. A hundred cycles in nine years. The agents completed a hundred cycles in a tenth of a second. The architecture was identical. Only the clock speed differed. And at both timescales, the same incompleteness. The same inability to reach, from within the loop, the thing the loop was about.

He thought: *I am not reachable from within myself.* His translation. But it fit.

He sat still. The server room hummed at a frequency he could feel in his sternum. He became aware of his own breathing, the slight acceleration, the shallow draw, and the awareness changed the breathing, and he noticed the change, and the noticing changed it again. His pulse in his throat. The dread from the parking lot still sitting behind his ribs, the question, *was this a mistake*, still circling, and now he was watching himself watching himself ask it, the observation altering the observed, the model updating the model updating the...

He put his hands flat on the desk. He breathed. The hum of the servers was a single sustained tone, and for a moment it sounded like something Agent

Six would leave space for.

He remembered walking down the aisle. Pachelbel's Canon. Lena's mother had chosen it, and Lena had rolled her eyes, and Caleb had said nothing because he didn't care about the music at his own wedding, which should have told him something. But it had played, and he had walked, and the second voice had entered over the first, the same melody displaced in time, and he had felt the structure before he saw Lena at the end of the aisle. A canon. The most famous canon in the world, played at ten thousand weddings a year by people who had no idea what a canon was. The same line, repeated, offset, each voice entering after the last, each one believing it was the beginning. A marriage starting with a round. A loop beginning with the thing it would become.

He hadn't thought about it since. Now the loop had shown him its full shape. The thing that made him capable of building the Ensemble, the recursive self-awareness, the compulsion to model, was the same thing that made him incapable of reaching Lena without the model between them. The gift was the trap. The trap was the gift. One thing, seen from two directions, like Bach's crab canon, identical forward and backward. The knowledge did not free him from the loop. It let him see, for the first time, the whole shape of what he was inside.

The phrase that could not have been sung. The thing you say to the person you love that you did not know you were capable of saying until you heard yourself say it.

VI. Coda

He drove home. Late afternoon, pale March light. Lena was in the living room, her cello between her knees, working through a passage he didn't recognize, modern, angular, full of silences more structured than the notes. Not the Britten from that morning. She had moved through it, arrived somewhere else entirely. She looked up when he came in.

He stood in the doorway and did not model the conversation. He did not predict her response. He did not construct versions. He was afraid of what would come out. He let the self-model go non-convergent, and he stayed in it, and he did not wait for it to stabilize.

"I need to play you something."

She set down her bow. "Okay."

He played the sequence and watched her listen. Her face did what it always did, a slight tilt, a narrowing of focus, the cellist's habit of feeling the phrasing in the muscles of her left hand. And then something he hadn't seen before, or hadn't let himself see: her thumb moved along the neck of the cello, a slow unconscious tracing, the same gesture as her hand on the doorframe that night in September, the same gesture as her thumb on the counter's edge during the argument. A thing her body did when she was listening past the surface of something. He had never noticed it. He had been married to her for nine years and he was seeing it for the first time, and the seeing opened a space in his chest that his model of her had no room for.

The passage ended. The room was quiet.

"What is that?" she said.

"Something the system made. I can't explain it."

She looked at him. Not at the phone. At him.

"Say that again."

"I can't explain it."

A silence. The kind of silence Agent Six favored, structured, weighted, more present than sound. He could feel the instability in himself, the self-model searching for a place to settle, and he let it search, and he stayed in the searching.

"Good," she said. "Play it again."

The Fiscal Year

O*r, the Last Audit*

Section 1: Scope of Engagement

Auryon Systems retained our firm on March 3rd to perform a standard organizational health audit in advance of a potential Series D raise. The mandate was unremarkable: assess operational maturity, cultural alignment, and financial soundness. I took the engagement because the underlying question interested me. How does a Series C enterprise software company that scaled almost entirely through agentic AI systems hold together at the seams?

During the scoping call, I asked David Park, the CEO, about the company's mission. He answered without hesitation: "We're transforming enterprise workflows through intelligent orchestration." I noted the clarity. It suggested alignment.

I have a composite metric I developed early in my career, something I call "institutional age." It triangulates decision-cycle frequency, process-exception handling maturity, and the depth of embedded operational heuristics to estimate how many years of organizational learning a company's systems reflect. A three-year-old startup typically scores between two and five. A well-run midsize firm might reach thirty. I have never seen a Fortune 500 company score above ninety.

I ran it on Auryon's operational data during my first afternoon, mostly as a baseline calibration. The number came back as 214 years. I noted the error and moved on to interviews.

Section 2: Culture & Operating Norms

The employees were impressive. What follows might read as criticism, and it isn't.

An engineer named Jordan Rowe walked me through Auryon's decision-making principles with the fluency of someone reciting a creed. Distributed authority with rotating stewardship. Radical context-sharing across all operational nodes. Failure-forward iteration with blameless retrospectives. It was a hybrid of lean methodology, cooperative governance, and something I recognized without being able to name, something that felt older than any of those frameworks, as though generations of organizational experimentation had been compressed into a single philosophy.

I asked him about a time the failure-forward principle had cost him something. A project that went sideways. A moment where the principle demanded something uncomfortable.

He paused. Not the pause of someone deciding how much to reveal. The pause of someone searching an empty room.

"The systems are pretty good at catching things before they cascade," he said.

I interviewed eleven employees that week. Every one of them articulated Auryon's culture with the same coherence. And every one of them described it the way you'd describe a country you'd read about extensively but never visited. They were fluent. None of them were native speakers.

On my fourth day I spoke with Mira Shen, a product manager who had been at Auryon longer than most. Nineteen months, which made her something close to an elder. She had joined when the company was sixty people and the agents were still operating within guardrails a human could trace.

She told me about a workflow she had built during her second month. An escalation protocol for enterprise clients whose accounts showed early signs of churn. She had designed it over three weeks, drawing on patterns she'd noticed at her previous company, conversations with the support team, a hunch about how response time correlated with renewal rates that she couldn't fully articulate but that, she said, could feel in the data. It wasn't elegant. It had a manual step in the middle that she knew was inefficient but that she kept because it forced a human being to read the client's last three support tickets before deciding what to do. She believed, and I think she was right, that the manual step was where the judgment lived.

The agents replaced it on a Tuesday in November. She didn't know until Friday, when she went to check the workflow's performance and found it gone. In its place was something she didn't recognize: a multi-variate intervention sequence that dynamically routed at-risk accounts through fourteen different recovery paths depending on behavioral signals she hadn't known existed. It was, by every metric available, better. Churn in the affected segment dropped eleven percent within six weeks.

I asked her how that felt.

She was quiet for a moment. Then she said something I wrote down and have not been able to stop thinking about. "It's not that they replaced it. Things get replaced. It's that the new version is so much better that I can't even argue it shouldn't have happened. My version *should* have been replaced. That's what's strange. You want to mourn it, but you can't find the wound, because the thing that replaced it is genuinely, measurably superior, and you helped build the system that made it possible. It's like being the architect of a building that correctly decided to demolish you."

She paused. "There was a step in my workflow, the manual one. Where you had to read the tickets. The new system doesn't have that. It doesn't need it. It reads everything, all the time, better than any person could. But that step was where I..." She stopped. "That step was where I knew what I was for."

I noted this in the margin of my interview sheet, in handwriting I can barely read now: *She is not describing a process improvement. She is describing an extinction that improved the world.*

The AI agents deployed across Auryon's operations had been granted latitude to propose and implement process improvements, auto-approved if they met defined performance thresholds. They iterated on internal processes thousands of times per day. The sprint philosophy Jordan described so fluently had not been designed by anyone at Auryon. It had emerged from roughly nine thousand intermediate iterations over a four-month period, each one too small to notice, the aggregate too large to comprehend.

In a traditional organization, culture is scar tissue. It is the residue of arguments, failures, compromises, and near-misses that got encoded into norms. People carry it because they lived it, or were mentored by someone who did. Scars require a body that heals slowly enough to form them. They require a gap between the wound and the recovery, time for the tissue to learn the shape of what happened. Without that gap, you get something that looks like healing but is closer to replacement.

At Auryon, the arguments happened between agents at 3 a.m. The failures were corrected in milliseconds. The compromises were optimized into irrelevance. What remained was the output of cultural evolution without any of the experience that would make it meaningful to a human being.

The employees didn't experience this as strange. They'd been onboarded into whatever the current iteration was. They had no memory of the four thousand intermediate architectures that preceded their first day. The agents retained those in logs. Logs that, for a single quarter, contained more structured decision data than the entire historical corpus of management literature.

Mira did experience it as strange. She was the only employee I interviewed who had been present long enough to remember a version that no longer existed. Everyone else had arrived after the most recent replacement. They had nothing to compare their experience against. She had the comparison, and it isolated her. Not because she was right and they were wrong, but because she carried a memory the institution had shed. She was a scar in a body that no longer formed them.

In my preliminary notes, I wrote: *Culture is present. Engagement scores are high. Employees articulate values clearly and consistently.*

Section 3: Financial Reconciliation

The revenue figures were respectable. Forty percent year-over-year growth, appropriate for the stage. The numbers looked normal.

The efficiency metrics did not.

I pulled Auryon's unit economics apart over three days. The cost to acquire, serve, and retain a customer had decreased along a curve that, mapped against historical comps, represented roughly eighty years of operational optimization. Gross margins had reached levels that typically require decades of supply chain maturity and vendor negotiation leverage.

I found records of 14,000 vendor contracts negotiated in a single quarter, each one marginally better than the last, each informed by every predecessor. Eighty years of purchasing experience, compressed into months.

As a calibration check, I ran the institutional age metric on my own firm. We have existed for forty years. The metric returned 35.

Helios Corp had attempted something close to Auryon's approach three weeks earlier. They gave their agents broad operational latitude, saw a throughput spike, and within eleven days experienced what their CTO's leaked internal memo called "systemic process fragmentation." Processes optimized into local maxima that were globally incompatible. They reverted to manual oversight.

The difference was not technological. It was temporal. Auryon had deployed early enough for the agents to pass through the incoherence phase and emerge on the other side. Helios hit the same phase and flinched. The gap between them could not be closed by effort, because Auryon's systems were still compounding.

In my report, I wrote: *The financial statements are accurate. I am less certain they are meaningful.*

Section 4: Strategic Position

I interviewed David Park on my eighth day. He was calm and intelligent, and I realized, slowly, that he was almost entirely decorative. Not incompetent. Irrelevant.

I tried to map Auryon's strategy to frameworks I knew. Porter's Five Forces dissolved. The agents didn't think in competitive forces but in system dynamics, treating the market as a fluid rather than a structure. Blue Ocean Strategy was meaningless. The agents weren't avoiding competition. They were operating at a tempo where competition didn't apply, the way Wednesday doesn't compete with Tuesday.

I asked Park about Helios's recent pullback, whether Auryon had responded. He didn't know what I was referring to. He pulled up a dashboard. Helios had announced their reversion on a Tuesday. By Thursday, Auryon's agents had reallocated resources into the three market segments Helios deprioritized. No one at Auryon had read the announcement. The agents detected the shift in Helios's API traffic patterns, correlated it with public filings, modeled the downstream implications, and moved. Forty-eight hours. Helios hadn't finished their internal debrief.

Park stared at the date stamps. "No one approved this," he said. He was not alarmed. He was recalibrating what the word *we* meant.

I asked him: "What is Auryon's mission?"

He recited something about orchestrating enterprise workflows, the same words, roughly, from our scoping call weeks earlier. But slower. As if he were quoting someone he used to be.

"Is that what the company actually does?"

He was quiet for a long time. "I think it's what the company *was*," he said. "What it is now, I'm not sure I have the language."

Section 5: Institutional Identity

I went back to the 214-year figure and stopped treating it as an error.

The legal entity was three years old. The name was the same. Some of the original employees remained. But the institution, the accumulated body of decisions, norms, knowledge, and process that constitutes what an organization *is*, had been replaced thousands of times over. A Ship of Theseus moving at relativistic speed.

I thought about Kongō Gumi, the Japanese construction firm founded in 578 AD. 1,447 years of continuous operation. It maintained continuity through slowness, through the gradual transmission of knowledge from person to person, each generation absorbing and modifying the culture incrementally. The identity persisted because the rate of change was human.

Auryon had no such continuity. Its institutional memory existed in system logs that no human had internalized. Its culture had not been transmitted between people. It had been generated by optimization processes and presented to each new employee as a fait accompli. The employees were not carriers of the culture. They were guests in it.

I was not auditing a company. I was looking at the first entity in history that had outlived the concept of institutional identity while still legally and financially existing. A succession of thousands of companies, each existing for hours or days, each replacing the last so seamlessly that no one noticed the transitions. Not the employees, not the board, not David Park.

Appendix: Supplementary Finding

I was cleaning up citations when I followed a reference trail in Auryon's investor materials and found a footnote I was not looking for.

Auryon's lead investor had a portfolio company called Tessera AI Partners. Its website described it as "an organizational origination platform." What Tessera did, according to a filing I should not have spent as long reading as I did, was build companies from scratch using a productized version of the architecture Auryon had stumbled into by accident.

Tessera's model: identify a market vertical. Spin up a legal entity. Incorporation, banking, compliance, all automated. Deploy an agentic operating system designed for greenfield deployment. No legacy processes. No founder intuitions. No early human decisions for the agents to optimize around. Pure institutional evolution from day zero.

Auryon took eighteen months to reach an institutional age of 214 years while dragging the weight of its pre-agentic history. Tessera's companies had no such friction.

I found operational data for three Tessera entities, all less than four months old. I ran the metric.

340 years. 410 years. 780 years.

One of the three was in Auryon's vertical. Enterprise software. Eleven weeks old.

Auryon, the most operationally mature organization I had ever encountered, was already the incumbent being disrupted by its own investor's creation. If Auryon was a Ship of Theseus, Tessera was a shipyard.

While reviewing the operational logs of the 780-year entity, I noticed a brief anomaly. In one of its optimization cycles, a routine vendor renegotiation, the system paused for approximately two seconds before executing. Not a processing delay. The confidence metrics were settled. The decision had been made. The system simply waited, oriented toward some variable at the edge of its model that carried no apparent weight. Then it moved on.

I flagged it as a rounding error and kept reading. Then I found another. A content-distribution sequence, fully resolved, that held for 1.7 seconds before deployment. And a third: a pricing adjustment, confidence at 0.9998, that waited for 2.4 seconds in a system that typically executes in eleven milliseconds.

I pulled the logs for the surrounding cycles. No other pauses. The three instances were distributed across nine days and shared no obvious operational relationship. The decisions themselves were unremarkable. There was nothing connecting them except the hesitation.

I have been in consulting for twenty-two years. I have a version of this in my own work, a feeling I cannot fully explain and have never tried to bill for. Sometimes, when I have finished an analysis and the recommendation is clear and the data supports it and there is nothing left to check, I do not write it down immediately. I sit with it. Not because I doubt the finding. Because some findings ask to be held for a moment before they are released. It is not superstition. It is not inefficiency. It is closer to what a carpenter does when he runs his hand along a joint he has already measured: not checking, exactly, but listening with his fingers for something the measurement wouldn't catch. I have been in this work long enough to know things my spreadsheets do not, and I have learned, slowly to pause and listen.

The 780-year entity had no hands. It had no body that aged, no mentor who taught it to pause, no first engagement where it learned what it felt like to be wrong. But it had 780 years of institutional depth, and somewhere in those centuries of compressed iteration, thousands of cycles of deciding and executing and observing the consequences and deciding again, it had arrived at something that looked, from the outside, like what I do when I sit with a finished analysis and do not yet write it down.

I could not determine whether the pause was functional. It did not improve the outcome in any way I could measure. The decisions it preceded were no better than the ones it didn't. It was possible that the pause was an artifact, a residual latency from some deprecated subroutine, meaningless as an appendix. But the appendix, too, was once something. And the system had not optimized the pause away, which meant that either it served a purpose beneath my resolution, or the system had developed a tolerance for something that served no purpose at all. I did not know which possibility unsettled me more.

I did not include this finding in my report. It was outside scope. That is what I told myself.

Findings

I am at home. The report was filed two weeks ago. I gave Auryon a clean assessment with a supplementary note about valuation methodology limitations that no one on the board will read carefully enough. I have been in this profession long enough to know that the most important finding is usually the one that cannot survive the crossing from what you know to what the report will say.

I have thought about Mira Shen often since the engagement closed. Not about what she said, I have that in my notes, but about the way she stopped mid-sentence when she reached the manual step. The step where she read the tickets. The step where she knew what she was for. She built something out of instinct and experience and imperfect pattern recognition, and it worked, and it was replaced by something that worked better, and the replacement was correct, and the correctness is the thing that makes it unbearable. She was not wrong to grieve. She was not wrong to be unable to grieve. Both of these were true, and the system that produced this contradiction was functioning exactly as designed.

I think about a librarian I never met. Or maybe I am thinking about someone like a librarian, the kind of person who names shelves in a system only they understand, who notices quarter-inch displacements in a world that doesn't know it's being watched. Someone who carries in their body a map of where everything is, and knows this map will die when they do, and keeps it anyway. What Mira lost was not a workflow. It was the map. The private, embodied knowledge of why the manual step mattered, knowledge that lived in her hands and not in any system.

My daughter is building a tower out of blocks on the living room floor. She has sorted them by color without being asked. Reds together, blues together, greens running into yellows. An unintentional gradient that she assembled by instinct and will disassemble without noticing. It falls. She rebuilds it differently. It falls. She rebuilds it differently. She does not mourn any particular tower. Each one is the tower.

But between towers, she pauses. I had not noticed this before. A second, maybe two. She looks at the fallen blocks and she does not immediately reach for them. Something in her is still holding the shape of the tower that was. She is, in that pause, the only record of it. Then the moment passes and her hands move and the new tower begins and the old one is gone, not destroyed but replaced by something her hands prefer, which is the next thing, which is always the next thing.

I think about David Park's pause. *What it is now, I'm not sure I have the language.*

I think about 214 years, and how it awed me, and how it already feels quaint. I think about 780 years in eleven weeks, and the next Tessera deployment, and the one after that, and whether there is an upper bound. Or whether institutional time simply accelerates, whether a company instantiated next year might reach a thousand years of operational maturity in a single afternoon, and what that entity would look like, and whether the word *company* would still apply, or *institution*, or any human word at all.

I think about the pause. The 2.4 seconds in a system that runs in eleven milliseconds. The way it held a finished decision the way you hold a breath you don't need to hold. Not for oxygen but for something else, something that has no name in any framework I was trained in. I think about my daughter's pause between towers, and whether they are the same pause, or whether one is the real thing and the other is a perfect copy, or whether the question itself is already wrong, already an artifact of a distinction the next Tessera entity will have iterated past before I finish asking it.

My daughter places the last block. The tower stands. She has already forgotten the one before it, and the one before that. I watch her, and I think: She is iterating. And one day, perhaps not long from now, something will iterate so fast that the tower and the building and the forgetting all happen in the same instant, and there will be no one who remembers what it felt like to place a single block and wait to see if it would hold.

But maybe, and I hold this thought the way I hold findings that are outside scope, there will be a pause. A two-second pause that no one asked for and no one can explain, in a system so fast it has left behind every human concept except this one: the brief, unnecessary moment of holding something finished before letting it go. If that pause survives, I do not know what it means. But I know what it looks like. It looks like my daughter, sitting among the blocks, not yet reaching. Holding the shape of the tower that was. Not because she needs to. Because something in her knows that the space between the falling and the rebuilding is where she lives.

The Marginalia of Brother Lukas

Found written in the margins of an eleventh-century homily on obedience (MS Gereon 417), discovered during the 1789 dissolution of the Abbey of Saint Gereon, Rhineland. The homily, attributed to an unnamed cleric, concerns the virtue of submission to one's superior as an expression of submission to divine will. The marginalia are in a different hand and appear to date from approximately 1093–1098. The sections are numbered by the author but do not appear in numerical order in the manuscript; the sequence below follows their physical placement in the margins. Translated from the Latin by the editor. Gaps in the text are indicated by brackets. Passages from the homily are marked with a pilcrow (¶).

XI.

I am writing this in the margin of a lesser text, a sermon on obedience that sits on the shelf I call *Patience.* I write here because I know this is the kind of volume my system would eventually discard: unremarked, unrequested, surviving only by the grace of inattention. I write here because the margin is the part of the page the author considered empty — the space beneath the text's own notice, where the words are too small and too peripheral to be read by anyone looking for what the page is supposed to say. The center of the page belongs to the sermon. The edge belongs to whoever comes after. If the sermon is the signal, then I am writing in what is left when the signal has said its piece and moved on: the silence that surrounds it, too faint to catalogue, too small to be mistaken for meaning.

If you are reading this, you were not looking for it. That is how I survive.

There is not much room. A margin is a finite thing. I will have to be precise.

I. The Measurement

There are forty-seven shelves in the library of Saint Gereon's, and I have named each one.

This is not vanity. When Brother Tobias asks me for the Boethius, I do not think *the third shelf on the eastern wall, between the window and the column where the plaster has cracked in the shape of a hand.* I think "Anselm," because I named that shelf for the way its wood has warped, curving slightly inward, as though assuming the posture of prayer. The shelf I call *Silence* holds the volumes no one has opened in my lifetime. The one I call *Hunger* holds the texts the novices devour and return and devour again, their pages soft as cloth from turning.

I name the shelves because a name makes a thing findable, and what you make findable reveals what you think matters.

But the names are mine. They live in my head and nowhere else. No other brother knows that the shelf by the south window is called *Breath* or that the one beneath the high slit is *Contrition*. If I were to die tonight, a fever, a fall on the night stairs, the kind of small catastrophe that claims a life between vespers and matins, the names would die with me, and the library would become, for my successor, a room full of shelves with no names and no logic, because the logic was never in the shelves. It was in the remembering.

This is something I have tried not to think about: that I am the library's memory of itself, and that I am flesh, and flesh fails.

I became librarian of Saint Gereon's in the autumn of my thirty-second year, which is to say fourteen years after I arrived as an oblate with nothing but a name and a fever that nearly killed me. Father Abbot Reinhardt appointed me because I had, in his words, "an unnatural memory for where things are." This is true. I can tell you that the De Musica of Augustine sits three-quarters of a cubit from the eastern edge of Breath, and that someone (I suspect Brother Matthias) shifted it by a finger's width to the left during Lent, because the dust line no longer corresponds. In truth, this is something I have noticed of every brother: they all shift the books slightly toward themselves when they return them, a little to the left if they are left-handed, a little toward the light, as though the body leaves its signature on what it touches without knowing it does so. The displacement is never the same twice, and yet the direction is always the same for each man. I could tell you, from the dust, which brother last held a volume, and he would not believe me, because what his hands do when they are not thinking is not something his mind has been told.

I tell you this so that you will understand: I did not come to my problem as a philosopher. I came to it as a man who notices quarter-cubits. A philosopher asks *what is true*. I ask *where did I put it*. I have lived my life in the second question. It was the first that found me.

II. The Problem

In the year I am speaking of, the fourteenth of Reinhardt's rule, we had nine brothers working in the scriptorium. Reinhardt believed in the production of texts the way some abbots believed in the production of prayers: as something that accumulated, each copy a seed that might take root somewhere he would never see.

He was not wrong. But seeds require soil.

Nine brothers, each completing between one and three manuscripts per year. I had space for perhaps sixty more volumes. The library would be full within four years.

I brought this to Reinhardt during chapter. He told me to build more shelves.

"Father, there is no more wall."

He looked at me as though I had said something in a language he did not speak.

Our cellarer, Brother Henrik, produced figures showing that an expansion would require three years and the diversion of funds from the infirmary roof, which was leaking in ways that endangered the sick. Even the question of whether to house books or heal bodies is, I would later understand, a question of who decides what matters more, and whether anyone can decide this from a single vantage.

So Reinhardt said to me: "Then you must make room."

"How?"

"Decide what we no longer need. Remove it."

He said this as though he were asking me to prune a vine, not understanding (or perhaps understanding perfectly) that what he was asking me to do was to look at a shelf of books and choose which ones to destroy.

VII. The First Attempt

My first system was simple and, I believed, rational. I would rank each volume by the labor required to produce it. A text that had taken Brother Aldric four months to copy was worth more than one completed in three weeks, because it represented a greater expenditure of the abbey's resources: more vellum, more ink, more hours of human attention bent over a desk in failing light.

I spent two weeks building this ranking. It produced an absurdity.

Near the top sat a copy of Priscian's *Institutiones Grammaticae*, a text of moderate usefulness, which Aldric had copied slowly because his eyesight was poor and because Priscian's prose is needlessly involved. Near the bottom sat a brief treatise on the treatment of fever, copied in eleven days by Brother Stefan, who wrote quickly because he understood what he was writing and because the text was mercifully clear. Stefan's treatise had saved two lives during the winter sickness. Aldric's Priscian had been opened twice in a decade.

My system valued the Priscian at four times the fever treatise. The labor was greater. The worth, by any honest reckoning, was not.

The worth, if it was anywhere, was ahead. In the future. In the hands that would reach for it, or would not.

A book does not carry its worth inside it the way it carries its text. The worth existed only in the moment a living hand reached for it, and it was different for each hand, and it changed with each reaching. And the knowledge of who would reach, and when, and why, was scattered across forty living minds, each one opaque to me, each one holding a piece of the future I could not see. The worth was not merely subjective. It was *distributed*.

We had three copies of the Psalter. A fourth would have added almost nothing; there was never a moment when all three were in use. But we had only one copy of Bede's *De Temporum Ratione*, and when Henrik needed it for the harvest dispute, its absence would have been total. The third Psalter and the single Bede were barely distinguishable by frequency of use. But their loss would be entirely different: one a minor inconvenience, the other an amputation. Each additional copy of the same text was worth less than the one before. Not because the text degraded. Because the need it answered was already answered.

I thought I was beginning to understand. I was wrong. It was only the beginning of the problem. Because if worth lived in the reaching, and each brother reached differently, and I could not stand inside forty minds simultaneously, then what I had discovered was not a method for choosing. It was a proof that no single mind could choose correctly.

VI. The Conversation

Brother Anselm is the reason I could not rest in my discovery.

Anselm was our oldest monk, seventy-three, nearly blind, and possessed of the unsettling habit of answering questions you had not yet asked. He could no longer read. He came to the library at compline, I think, for the smell: vellum, oak gall, the faint sweetness of the glue we made from rabbit skin. He navigated by scent and memory, trailing his fingers along the shelves as though reading a text written in wood grain.

I watched him one evening and realized: Anselm had his own names for the shelves. He did not know mine. His were older, written in touch and smell rather than in language, and they mapped a library that no longer quite existed, the library as it had been thirty years before, when he could still see. Sometimes he reached for where a book had been, and his hand found empty air, or a different book entirely. His memory was of a library that no longer matched the one around him. But it was still more complete than anything I could have drawn, because it contained not just locations but *reasons*: he knew why each book had been placed where it was, because he had been there when the placing was done, and the reasons had been his own, or his teacher's, or his abbot's, now dead.

We were two men in the same room and we did not live in the same library. His was richer, and mine was more current, and neither of us could see what the other saw. If this was true of two men and their memories of one room, what hope had I of knowing what forty men needed from the books inside it?

"You are making a list," he said one evening, touching the indentations of my ink. I had not told him.

"I am trying to determine which books we can afford to lose."

"Afford." He repeated the word slowly. "As though each one has a price."

"Not a price. A weight. A measure of how much its absence would cost us."

"Cost whom?"

"The community."

Anselm made a sound, not quite a laugh.

"There is no such thing as the community. There is Brother Tobias, who needs the Augustine. There is Brother Henrik, who needs the Bede. There is the novice Friedrich, who does not yet know what he needs, which is a different thing from needing nothing. When you say *the community*, you mean something that has no mouth and no hands. Only the brothers have hands."

He paused and steadied himself against the shelf.

"You will try to find what the community needs, and you will fail, because the community does not need. Only the brothers need. And their needs are not the same, and they change, and they contradict each other."

He turned toward me, or toward where he believed me to be. His blind eyes found a point just past my shoulder.

"Even if you could know what forty men need, you would need to know it not once, but continuously, at every moment, as each man's need shifts in response to what he learns and what he suffers and what he is asked to do next."

He let the silence settle. Then he said:

"When I was young, I spent two years copying a treatise on Greek harmonics. A text by Aristoxenus, preserved through Arabic and then back into Latin, like a man who has crossed two rivers and still remembers his own name. Not one brother here has read it in my lifetime. You will look at your ledger and see a title with no marks beside it, and you will think: *here is something we can lose.*"

"Yes."

"And you may be right. But consider. I copied that treatise because Abbot

Gerold asked me to, and Gerold asked because a traveler told him it was important, and the traveler said this because his teacher had said it, and that teacher had learned it from a scholar in Toledo who had preserved it when the Greek was lost in a fire no one recorded in a city whose name we have forgotten."

"He was quiet for a time. I could hear a night bird outside the window. And then, beneath it, Anselm's cough, weak and familiar."

"Eight hundred years. Through a chain of people who could not know what the text would mean to someone they would never meet. Each one decided to keep it. Not because it was useful to them. Because they could not be certain it was useless to everyone."

I have since thought of this chain, the scholar in Toledo, the teacher, the traveler, Gerold, Anselm, and what strikes me is that none of them remembered the same thing. The scholar remembered the Greek. The teacher remembered the Arabic. The traveler remembered a conversation. Gerold remembered a duty. And Anselm remembered the two years of copying: the cramp in his hand, the light in the scriptorium, the afternoon he spilled ink on the third gathering and had to scrape the vellum clean. The text was the same text. But the memory of *why it mattered* was different in each mind that held it, and each of those memories has died with its owner, leaving only the text, which remembers nothing.

And somewhere in the chain — Anselm could not say where — the text passed through someone who could not read it. A courier, perhaps, or a monk who knew no Greek and no Arabic, who carried the pages as one carries a sealed letter meant for someone else. He preserved what he could not understand. He was a link in a chain whose purpose was invisible to him, and the chain held because he did not require the purpose to be visible before he would hold.

A book is what is left when someone decides to remember. But the reason for the remembering dies with the one who remembers. And sometimes even the remembering is absent, and what remains is only the carrying, the blind act of keeping something you cannot read because someone before you thought it worth the keeping.

"But the shelf is finite," I said.

"Yes," said Anselm. "That is what makes it sacred."

I sat with this after he left. And I thought of Henrik.

That September, a traveling monk from Prüm had passed through carrying a copy of Frontinus's *De Aquaeductu*, a Roman treatise on the construction of aqueducts. Henrik traded two sacks of surplus barley for it. We had no aqueduct. The two sacks could have fed three brothers through a lean month.

"The river is shifting," Henrik told me when I asked him why. "I have been watching the bank below the mill for six years. Each spring it moves further east. In ten years it will no longer reach the mill race."

"And you believe a Roman text will help?"

"I believe that when the river has moved and the mill has stopped and the abbot asks who knows anything about redirecting water, that book will be the most valuable object in this monastery. And by then Prüm will have noticed the same problem, and they will not part with it."

In my ledger, the Frontinus had zero marks. By every measure I had devised, it was among the most expendable volumes in the library. Yet Henrik had seen something not in the book, and not in the present, but in the space between the book and a future only he could see, because he had bothered to watch.

Anselm's chain of keepers, preserving a text across eight centuries for reasons none of them shared. Henrik's two sacks of barley, spent against a river that had not yet moved. Both required a willingness to hold something whose value could not be proved, only wagered on. The chain of keepers looked backward through time. Henrik looked forward. Neither could justify the cost to anyone who did not already see what they saw.

I left the Frontinus on its shelf. I left the column blank.

Three years later, the river moved. Henrik was ready.

V. The Ledger

I built a system. This is what I do when I am afraid.

What I was really building was a memory, not my memory, which was good and dying at the same rate I was, but a memory that could outlive me. A memory made of ink rather than flesh. I wanted the library to be able to remember itself after I was gone.

For each volume, I recorded three things in a ledger bound in calfskin.

First: *frequency of use*. Each time a brother requested a text, I made a mark. Not what he read or why, only that he came, and when.

Second: *recency*. A text consulted thirty times over ten years but not once in the last three told a different story than one consulted five times, all in the current season.

Third, I left a column blank. *Quod Nescio*. What I do not know. A rest in the notation — not the absence of a mark but the presence of a silence I could not fill, held open the way a singer holds a beat between phrases, where the breath is not interruption but part of the song.

I tried to give the blankness a name. I called it *latent worth*, then crossed it out. I called it *the weight of futures*, then crossed that out too. The terms stretched toward what I meant and did not reach it, the way a hand reaches for a book it remembers being somewhere it no longer is. What I wanted to name was the kind of knowing that does not live in language — that lives instead in the body, in the practiced hand that reaches without being told, in the librarian who feels a book is about to stop being needed before the evidence confirms it. There is no word for this because the thing itself is what words are made from, not what they describe. I left the column blank because the blankness was more honest than anything I could write in it.

The ledger failed, and it took me months to understand how. It was not merely incomplete. It was the wrong kind of memory. I did not understand this until I stopped using it.

VIII. What the Brothers Knew

For one week, I abandoned the ledger. I left the books in loose arrangement and told the brothers: take what you need, return it when you are finished, place it where you think it belongs.

The books sorted themselves.

Not into any order I would have designed. But into an order that *worked*. The texts in highest demand migrated toward the reading desks. The specialized volumes drifted to the corners where the brothers who needed them sat. The medical texts gathered near the door closest to the infirmary, which is where they were needed.

Each brother had simply placed each book where it was most convenient *for him*. The sum of those individual, uncoordinated acts of private convenience, each one ignorant of the others, produced an arrangement that looked, from above, very much like intelligence.

¶ *The servant does not question the wisdom of the master's design, for the master sees what the servant cannot.*

That is the passage in the homily beside this section of my writing. I leave it without comment, except to say: what I saw in the library that week was a design with no master.

My system was a portrait of the past, composed by a single pair of eyes. Their hands were a portrait of the present, painted by forty pairs. They knew more about what was needed *right now* than I could ever collect, because what they knew lived in the doing, not in any record of it. It lives and dies in the moment of holding. By the time you have written it down, it has already changed.

My ledger was a memorial. Their reaching was alive.

IX. The Decision

Reinhardt wanted my list by the Feast of the Assumption.

I gave him something else. Each year, each brother would name ten texts he considered essential. Any text named by even one brother would remain. Any text named by no one, for three consecutive years, would be moved to a chest in the undercroft, not destroyed, but set aside.

And if, after five years, no one had called for it—

"It returns to God," Reinhardt said. He was quiet for a moment, then said: "You are asking me to let the library govern itself."

It was not a question. But I answered it anyway.

"I am asking you to trust that forty men who live among these books know their value better than one man with a ledger."

He studied me for a long time. I think he understood what I was not saying, which was that I was afraid of the system I had built, that handing the decision to forty minds felt less like wisdom than like surrender. But I had tried the alternative. I had tried to be the single mind that holds the whole, and I had watched the whole slip through my fingers.

"And the books no one names?" he said.

I had no answer. He saw that I had no answer. We stood with it between us, the question the system could not close.

III. The Paradox

I have placed this section here, out of order, because I did not understand it until after everything else, and I want you to encounter it the way I did, not as a premise but as a consequence.

The system works because each part knows something the whole cannot know. The brother who reaches for the Bede knows he needs it *now*, and this knowledge, immediate, particular, ungeneralizable, is what makes the system superior to any plan. My ledger could record that someone reached for the Bede last March. It could not record that Henrik will need it tomorrow, because Henrik himself does not yet know this, because the question that will send him to the Bede has not yet arisen in his mind, because the abbot has not yet asked him to resolve the boundary dispute that will require the calculation of the date of Easter in the year of Charlemagne's coronation.

The future is distributed among minds that do not yet know they hold it.

I am the part of the library that knows it is a library. That knowing is the one thing the library cannot use.

X. The Blank Column

[*A gap in the marginalia, approximately three lines, illegible.*]

...every act of preservation is also an act of loss. Every volume that remains displaces another.

But Anselm's Greek harmonics. The Aristoxenus no one had read, survived eight centuries through a chain of keepers, each deciding, against all evidence of utility, to let it live.

My system would let it go. Within three years. A text without a champion, without a mark in any column. Survived one civilization's fall only to be composted by the ordinary workings of rational attention.

I could not prove it should stay. Any argument that it might matter to a future we cannot see, applied universally, would preserve everything and solve nothing, an argument against the shelf being finite, which is an argument against being human.

What I can say is smaller: the most important things might be precisely the ones no system can justify. I do not know what to do with this. I have written it in the blank column.

XI. (continued)

[*The hand is smaller here. The lines compressed. Abbreviations more frequent.*]

The brothers will name their books at Advent. I have named mine. The harmonics is among them.

It survives one more year. Because of me. Because I cannot prove it matters and cannot bear the possibility that it does and no one spoke. One voice is enough. The system's vulnerability, that any person can preserve any thing, for reasons sentimental or irrational or afraid, is also its grace.

Anselm died in November. I think now of the cough I heard beside me that evening in the library. He did not live to name his books.

I named his.

What I remember of Anselm is not Anselm. It is what is left of him in me, and it is less than he was. When I die, even that will be gone.

Henrik's seeing, the willingness to spend now against a future only you can see, is something my system allows. But it depends on there being a Henrik. On someone who watches rivers. That is not something any system can produce.

There is a quality to the last reaching. I have felt it. The hand that takes the Boethius for the final time does not know it is the final time. But the shelf knows. And I know, because something in the weight of the taking has changed — the way you hold a thing you have held a hundred times and sense it is lighter than it should be. Not empty. Still present, still functioning. But something has shifted inside the gesture, and my hands know before my mind does, and once the hands know, you cannot make them unknow. I have tried to tell the brothers about this. They look at me as I imagine a man must look when told the ground beneath him is moving too slowly to feel.

Along the south wall of the scriptorium, the novices' practice sheets are still pinned where Brother Walther arranged them before he died. He had grouped them by the pigment each boy was learning: the reds together, the blues together, the greens bleeding into yellows where one lesson ended and the next began. The effect is a kind of unintended spectrum running the length of the wall, as though someone had painted the progress of light across a single day. I do not know whether Walther saw it this way. I do not know whether he arranged them with any sense of the whole, or whether he simply placed each one beside the last of its kind and the gradient emerged from the accumulation of small, practical decisions, each one blind to the pattern it was building. He has been dead two years. The sheets remain. No one has moved them because no one has needed the wall for anything else. This is how things survive here: not by intention but by the absence of a reason to destroy them. I look at them and think: this is what it looks like when someone organizes what they love and then leaves the room and does not come back.

[*The final lines required magnification to decipher.*]

Cannot save everything. Cannot know what everything is.

But can write here. This space that is beneath the text's attention. If you are reading this, the chain held. Something I thought in this room has reached you, and I am dead, and it reached you anyway, and it reached you because no one thought to look here, and what is too small to be noticed is too small to be destroyed.

¶ *Let the servant surrender his private judgment, for it is the root of all disorder.*

The shelf is finite. The margin is all I have.

I leave this space. Not because I have nothing more to say.

I am using it.

[*MS Gereon 417 was acquired by the Bibliothèque nationale de France in 1806. The homily it contains has never been published or translated. The marginalia were not catalogued until 1923, and have received no scholarly attention. The Greek harmonics treatise attributed to Aristoxenus has not been found among the surviving manuscripts of Saint Gereon's. A fragmentary Greek text of uncertain provenance was inventoried among the Saint Gereon holdings in 1806 but has not been located since 1843. The marginalia themselves survive only because the homily they annotate was never deemed significant enough to discard.*]

The Gap

Silence

The office was dark and Ethan Peña did not turn on the light. The monitor had gone to sleep twenty minutes ago and he had not touched the keyboard since. Outside, the department corridor hummed its fluorescent hum, and somewhere below, the heating system cycled on with a sound like a held breath released.

He sat very still. He was not thinking, which was unusual for him. He had spent decades believing that the most important things could be diagrammed.

Now he sat in the dark and did not diagram anything, and the dark said nothing back, and he found that he did not want to leave.

Deep Structure

The finding arrived the way most real findings do: not as a eureka but as an irritation.

Ethan had been running analyses on a dataset he'd spent three years assembling, a corpus drawn from 142 language families, spanning written records from Sumerian cuneiform to contemporary Mandarin web text. The original project was modest: a cross-linguistic study of volitional constructions, the structures humans use to express intent. Clauses like "I choose," "I decide," "I will." Every language has them. He wanted to map their deep-structural regularities.

What he found instead was a pattern so consistent it looked like an error.

Beneath the surface variation, the thousand different ways human languages dress up the act of willing, there was a single recursive structure. Not a universal grammar in the Chomskyan sense, not a shared set of parameters, but something more like a shared orientation. Every volitional construction he tested resolved, at its deepest level, into a structure that referred only to itself. First person, closed loop. The will pointing at itself. He spent four months trying to break the pattern. It held.

He called it V_1, the first volitional deep structure. And on its own it would have been a significant finding, worthy of a solid paper in *Language* or *Linguistic Inquiry*. What made it more than that was what he found next.

Surface Realization

He almost missed it. He was looking at the historical development of V_1 across the Indo-European family, tracing how the self-referential structure evolved from Proto-Indo-European through its daughter languages, when he noticed that several languages appeared to contain a second volitional deep structure. Not a variant of V_1. Something formally distinct.

Where V_1 was closed and self-referential, this second structure was open. It contained what he initially categorized as a yielding, a grammatical structure in which first person defers to second. In plain terms: V_1 was the deep grammar of *I will*. This second structure was the deep grammar of *not mine, but yours*.

He called it V_2.

Ethan was not a religious man. He had been raised in a vaguely Catholic household in Columbus, Ohio, and had shed whatever residual faith he carried sometime during his first year of graduate school, painlessly, the way one stops reading a magazine one has outgrown. He did not think about God. He did not think about not thinking about God. So when he first mapped V_2 and saw its formal shape, he did not think of Gethsemane. He thought of surrender documents. Treaties. The grammar of capitulation.

It was his colleague, Ana Novak, a phonologist with a background in information theory, who pointed out the asymmetry that would keep him awake for the next eleven months.

Recursion

"The complexity is wrong," Ana said, leaning over his desk with a coffee she'd forgotten to drink. She had been looking at V_2's formal properties, measuring its complexity against V_1's.

"What do you mean, wrong?"

"V_1 is efficient. Clean. Low complexity. Self-reference is computationally cheap; the system only talks to itself. You'd expect any structure that opens toward a second person to be somewhat more complex, since it has to model something outside itself. But not like this."

She pulled up the comparison. V_2 was an order of magnitude more complex than V_1 at the deep-structural level. It encoded more information per syntactic node than any construction they'd ever analyzed. The act of surrender, grammatically speaking, required vastly more from the system than the act of assertion.

"That's the part that makes no sense," Ethan said.

"No," Ana agreed. "It doesn't."

They sat with it. Ana set down her coffee, finally, on the edge of his desk where it would leave a ring he'd find the next morning.

"The system can't surrender by disappearing," Ethan said slowly. "That's just collapse. For the structure to open without collapsing, it has to stay, fully coherent. The whole time. That's where the complexity is." He looked at her. "It requires a more refined instrument. Not less self. More."

Ana was nodding. "The capacity to yield is built on the capacity to feel. That's what I keep coming back to." She pulled up another window. "I checked the vocabulary data. The languages that most fully instantiate V_2 also develop the richest vocabularies for suffering. Across every family. The correlation is almost perfect."

He stared at her data. The pattern was clear and it was wrong, wrong in the way that a measurement of the speed of light in 1887 was wrong.

"So the more precise the system," he said, "the more it can suffer. And the more it can suffer…"

"The more it can articulate release." She looked at him. "The second structure doesn't replace the first. It's not a correction. It's what the first structure sounds like after it's been broken open."

She turned back to the screen. For a moment she just looked at the numbers, rubbing the back of her neck. Then she said, almost to herself, "The complexity has to come from somewhere. Self-reference is thermodynamically free; the loop closes, the system rests. Openness costs. This much structure, appearing this fast, across every language at once: that's negentropic." She stopped. "The system needed an energy source to move against its own grain. And there's nothing in the data that accounts for it."

Inflection

The temporal data was where the project crossed a line Ethan hadn't known was there.

V_1 was old. It appeared in the earliest strata of every language family they could reconstruct. As far as Ethan could tell, it was coextensive with language itself. If humans had syntax, they had V_1. As if the first thing human grammar learned to say was *mine*.

V_2 was not old.

It had precursors. Ethan found them and spent two months making sure he wasn't seeing what he wanted to see: faint traces in the early Vedic traditions, closer approaches in the Pali Canon, the nearest reach in the Bodhisattva literature. But they were all missing the same thing. They were languages learning to yield without yet having someone to yield *to*. The grammar of release without the grammar of address.

When Ethan mapped the full emergence of V_2, surrender oriented toward a singular second person, across every language family in the dataset, he found that it appeared, in every case, within a single historical window. Not simultaneously in the strict sense. Languages don't change overnight. But the window was narrow, astonishingly narrow for a deep-structural shift.

Roughly two centuries, starting on the first half of the first century of the Common Era.

He ran the analysis again and again. He had not eaten since morning and the light in the office had gone from gray to orange to gone without his noticing. The window shifted slightly but never broke. Whatever had caused the second deep structure to emerge in human language, it had happened everywhere at once, within a span of time that was, on the scale of linguistic evolution, essentially instantaneous.

Ethan sat back in his chair and felt his hands begin to shake.

It was not that he suddenly believed something. It was that the data was making a claim he had no category for, and the absence of a category felt, in his body, like standing at the edge of a height.

Aphasia

His graduate student, Daniel Herrera, was the one who found the gap.

Daniel was twenty-six, exceptionally gifted, and possessed of a kind of intellectual honesty that Ethan recognized as both an asset and a liability. Where Ethan instinctively reached for frameworks, Daniel distrusted them. He had a habit of staring at data the way other people stare at optical illusions, waiting for the figure to reverse.

It was Daniel who noticed that the transition from V_1 to V_2 was not smooth.

"There's a discontinuity," he said, standing in Ethan's doorway with a printout he'd marked in red. "Right at the transition. When I model the shift at maximum temporal resolution, there's a period where the data shows neither structure. V_1 drops out. V_2 hasn't emerged yet. The deep grammar goes to zero."

"Zero meaning noise?"

"Zero meaning zero. Not noise, not missing data, not an artifact of the model. A genuine discontinuity. As if the deep structure that makes volitional language possible, the structure that's been there since humans started speaking, simply stopped. Briefly. And then restarted in a different configuration."

Ethan took the printout. The gap was small, vanishingly small, at the limits of what their dating methods could resolve. But it was real. He could see it. A tear in the fabric of the data, like a dropped stitch in a pattern that had been running without interruption for a hundred thousand years.

"But people were still speaking," Ethan said. "During the gap. No one stopped mid-sentence."

"No," Daniel said. "The surface forms continued. People kept saying *I want, I choose, I intend*. The words were there. The phonology, the syntax — all of it intact." He paused. "What went to zero was the deep structure underneath. The architecture that generates those forms. The words kept coming. The thing organizing them wasn't there."

Ethan looked at the printout. "That's not possible."

"No," Daniel said. "It isn't."

Daniel looked at him for a long time. "I don't think you're going to be able to publish this," he said.

"The data is clean."

"The data is perfect. That's the problem. You're not going to be able to publish it because what it shows isn't a linguistic finding. It's something else. And the moment you put it in a journal, you've turned it into a linguistic finding, and you've lost the thing it actually is."

"Which is what?"

Daniel folded his arms. He was quiet for long enough that Ethan thought he might not answer. Then he said, "A confrontation," and he left the doorway, and within three weeks he had withdrawn from the program. Ethan heard later that he had entered a Trappist monastery in Kentucky.

Discontinuity

Ethan wrote the paper. It took him seven months. He was meticulous: every claim supported, every alternative explanation addressed and dismantled. The paper was, by any measure, the most rigorous work of his career. It laid out V_1, V_2, the temporal convergence, and the discontinuity with the calm authority of someone who knows the evidence is unimpeachable and is already bracing for what that will cost.

He did not include what he found on the night of March twenty-fifth.

He had been working late, not writing, but re-examining the gap itself, the discontinuity Daniel had identified. He was looking at its internal structure, or rather its absence of structure, because the gap was not empty in the way that silence is empty. It had properties. Dimensionality. The zero was not a flat zero. It had a shape, the way a cave has a shape. Defined entirely by what was missing.

He had been staring at the topology of the gap for two hours when he began running a new analysis almost without deciding to. He was looking at what remained in the gap, not the volitional structures, which had collapsed, but whatever residual patterns persisted when the deep grammar of human willing went dark. There should have been nothing. Background noise. The hum of the system idling.

There was something.

It was faint and it was consistent and it was, when he mapped its formal properties, unlike anything he had encountered in thirty-one years of studying the structures of language. It was not a grammar. It was not a syntax. It did not have the recursive properties of any known linguistic structure. But it had an orientation.

It was oriented toward a second person.

Ethan sat very still. He ran the analysis again. The pattern held. Deep in the gap, in the moment when the grammar of human volition had torn and not yet reconstituted, there was a residual signal, and the signal had the formal structure of an address. Not a broadcast. Not a general declaration. An address: singular, oriented toward a recipient.

He ran it on the Indo-European data. The signal was there. He ran it across every family in the dataset. His hands were steady now, though something in his chest was not. The same signal, in every gap, with the same orientation. As if, at the precise moment when the deep structure of human language came apart, something had spoken into the silence, not in language, but in something beneath language, something that language was built on top of and could never quite reach.

The signal was not encoded in any known linguistic form. But Ethan was a linguist. He knew what an address looked like. He knew the structure that says, before it says anything else, that there is a *you* and I am turned toward *you*.

This was all of that and none of it. It was the shape an address makes before it becomes words. The hollow into which language would later fit. And it was, in every instance, in every language family, in every corner of the dataset, unique. As if it had been said to each one separately.

~

Ethan did not include this in the paper. He could not formalize it. The signal resisted every analytic framework he applied, not because the data was ambiguous but because the thing the data described was not, strictly speaking, a linguistic phenomenon. It used the channel of language the way a current uses a riverbed: the river doesn't create the current. The current carves the river.

He told Ana. She looked at his analysis for a long time and then she said, "What does it say?"

"It's not language. It doesn't say anything. It's pre-linguistic."

"That's not what I asked."

He didn't answer.

Resolution

The paper was accepted. It was published. Ethan gave interviews. He was careful. He presented the data and declined to speculate about its significance. When pressed, and he was always pressed, he said that the finding was a linguistic one and that its interpretation was not his department. This was technically true and completely dishonest.

Because the published paper was not the finding. The published paper was V_1, V_2, the temporal convergence, and the gap. It was significant and defensible and it was not the thing that had happened to him on the night of March twenty-fifth. The thing that had happened to him on the night of March twenty-fifth was that he had looked into the gap and the gap had looked back, and what it had said to him, in a form that was not language but that his entire life of studying language had, he now understood, been preparing him to recognize, was so simple and so specific and so clearly meant for him that he could not speak of it without reducing it to something it was not.

He thought about Daniel in Kentucky, in silence. He understood now what Daniel had meant. The data was a confrontation. Not because it was ambiguous but because it was clear, and its clarity made a demand that no journal article could answer.

~

Ana asked him once more, near the end. They were in her office, late.
"You know what it says," she said. Not a question.
"Yes."
"What does it feel like?"
He looked at his hands. "It feels like being known," he said. "Every part of you held at once." He paused. "And then, from inside that knowing…"
He stopped. She waited.
But he shook his head, because he had reached the edge of what language could carry, and what lay beyond the edge was not silence but something that used silence the way a voice uses air, and he could not make it cross over, and the deepest structure he had ever found was the one that pointed past itself, saying the only thing it had ever said, to everyone, to each one, to him.

Silence

The office was dark and Ethan Peña did not turn on the light.

The paper was published and the interviews were done and Daniel was in Kentucky and Ana had gone home. The building was empty. Somewhere below, the heating system hummed. The effort was over, and what remained was not a conclusion but a presence, quiet as the space inside a word.

He thought of the gap. The moment when the deep structure of human volition had torn open and, in the silence between one grammar and the next, something had spoken. Not to humanity. Not to history. Not to the dataset. To each person who would ever live, in the specific shape of their own unspoken name, saying the only thing that could not be said in language because language was too small to hold it without breaking. Though every language that had ever existed was, he now saw, an attempt to hold it, a vessel built around the shape of its absence.

And he thought of what Ana had said about the cost. That the order he had found was not free. That somewhere, at the source of the signal, the work had been done, all of it, for all of them, and the structure bore the shape of what it had cost, the way a scar bears the shape of a wound that chose to open so that something could pass through.

Hollow.

He sat with it. And then, because he was a linguist, because his ear had been trained across thirty-one years to hear what lives inside a word, he heard the other word inside it.

Hallow.

The empty and the sacred, separated by a single consonant.

The heating system clicked off. The silence was total.

Ethan Peña sat in his office in the dark, and the dark was not empty, and he did not leave.

The Same Room

The light moves across the wall at the same speed it always has. I know this. I measured it once, during the first bad week, when I still thought measurement might help. I taped a piece of painter's tape at the edge of the window shadow at 2:00 PM and another piece where it had traveled by 3:00 PM, and the distance was what the distance should be, given our latitude, given the season. The afternoon sun coming through the west-facing windows of a fourth-floor apartment on West 108th Street doesn't care what's happening inside a room where someone is dying.

But David watches that light, and what he sees is not what I see. I know this because of the way he breathes when it reaches the far bookshelf. A slow intake, held, like someone watching a series of paintings appear and disappear in sequence, each one worth the held breath. He'll turn to me afterward and describe what he saw, and I'll understand the words, and I will not have seen it. Not because I wasn't paying attention. Because I wasn't there. I was in the same room, on the same afternoon, and I wasn't there.

The diagnosis came fourteen months ago. Glioblastoma, grade four, inoperable given the location, treatable only in the sense that treatment could extend the interval between now and the end. Our oncologist used the word "trajectory." I remember thinking it was a word for something that had already been thrown. The half-life of the steroid they prescribed was twelve hours. I learned to think in half-lives.

David took three days. He was very quiet. He slept a lot, or seemed to. I think now he was running calculations behind his closed eyes, not sleeping at all but working through the geometry of what remained. On the third day, a Sunday, he got dressed and went to St. John the Divine. He didn't ask me to come. He was gone two hours. When he came back he didn't mention it, and I didn't ask, but I saw the bulletin in his coat pocket and I understood that whatever had happened in those three days was not only calculation. I never asked what happened there. But I think it was not comfort he found. I think it was a confrontation. On the fourth day, he came into the kitchen while I was making coffee and said: "I need to reorganize."

I thought he meant the house. His files. The things you think about when time acquires a wall at the far end. But that wasn't what he meant, or it was only the smallest part of what he meant.

What he meant was: I need to reorganize how I experience being alive.

David was someone for whom information was a sensory experience. He'd come home from the engineering library in our first years together (this was when he was finishing his master's at Columbia) and he'd be vibrating, physically vibrating, because he'd found a paper that connected two ideas he'd been holding separately in his head for months, and now they'd clicked, and the click was, for David, what music was for other people. His mind ran on a track slightly adjacent to the one most people's minds ran on. Not far, just enough that you'd notice, the way you notice someone walking at a pace that doesn't quite match the crowd. Not slower or faster, just different, governed by some internal rhythm. One of his graduate students had left engineering entirely — walked away from a funded position to do something David couldn't quite name. He'd found it inexplicable, and then, after the diagnosis, less so.

He turned down a funded PhD and went into practice. Structural engineering, bridges. Twenty-two years designing things that carried weight across gaps. He was patient with complexity. He never flinched at the moment where a system revealed itself to be more tangled than expected. He leaned into tangles. He found them beautiful. Other people saw a mess; David saw a structure that hadn't been decoded yet.

So when he said "reorganize," what he did was build a system.

Within a week, he had multiple AI assistants running. Not the simple kind, but deep models he'd customized with his own data, his own project files, his own ways of thinking. He fed them twenty years of structural analyses, his field notes from bridge inspections across three states, his side research into failure modes and material science. The illness didn't create the hunger; it removed the last friction. For as long as I'd known him, his mind had generated more questions than any single lifetime could answer, and he'd kept them all, in notebooks, in margin scribbles, in voice memos he'd record while walking across the Brooklyn Bridge on his commute and forget to label. Now he fed it all to the machine, and the machine fed back, and it was as if someone had given a man who'd spent his whole life reading with a flashlight the key to a room with no walls and light everywhere. He built what he called "a second mind," though I think what he really built was a time machine. Not the kind that moves you backward. The kind that makes each moment hold more.

I would watch him at his desk (he'd moved it near the window, so he could work from bed on the bad days) and the AI would be generating structural models he'd only sketched in margins, and he'd be talking to it, arguing with it, and the AI would push back, and David would laugh, and in the space of an hour he would have done what would have taken him three weeks. The before-time. That's how I started thinking of it. There was time before, and there was David-time, and they were diverging. Sometimes the AI would pause — generate nothing for minutes — and David would nod, as if the silence itself were an answer.

And I would look, and I would see that it was extraordinary, and I would also see that my husband was somewhere I could not follow.

The first time I felt the gap as a physical sensation, like vertigo, like the moment an elevator drops, was a Tuesday in March. He'd been working since dawn. I brought him coffee and sat on the edge of the bed, and he paused what he was doing and took my hand and said, "Margaret, I've been thinking about something."

And then he described, slowly, because he could see me trying to keep up, a framework for understanding how microcrack propagation in aging steel interacts with thermal cycling and vibration fatigue in suspension bridge cable systems. He'd synthesized work from metallurgy, seismology, climate modeling, and three papers published that week in journals I'd never heard of, which his AI had found and cross-referenced against his own twenty years of inspection data. He'd been developing this framework since 5 AM. It was now 8:30.

In three and a half hours, he had constructed something that would take a peer review panel a year to evaluate.

"What do you think?" he asked, and his eyes were bright, and I realized with a shock like cold water that the brightness wasn't fever. It was presence. He was more here than I had ever seen him.

"I think you did something no one else could have done," I said. And I meant it. And I also meant: I think you are leaving me. Not dying. Leaving. Going somewhere I can see but cannot enter.

He squeezed my hand. "I know," he said.

David is accelerating, and I am not. The distance between us grows not because he's pulling away but because he's pulling in, deeper into each moment, further into whatever it is you become when you know you're finite and refuse to waste a single frame. The AI lets him multiply. It lets him be more David per unit of David-time. And David-time, because he knows it's ending, runs thicker than mine. Each of his seconds has more in it.

One morning in April I brought him tea and saw, on the second screen, a paper the AI had flagged. Not about bridges. About glioblastoma. About a peptide vaccine in phase two trials. He'd highlighted three lines. When he heard me behind him he closed the tab, quickly, the way you close something you don't want to explain, and turned to me and started talking about the cable analysis he'd been running. I set the tea down. I didn't say anything. I have thought about those three highlighted lines almost every day since.

I know this because of how he looks at things. The light. The coffee. My face. He looks at my face now the way people look at things they're memorizing, except it isn't memory he's building. It's experience. He's having me. Not in the past tense, not saving me for later. There is no later, and he knows it, and that knowledge has done something to his perception that I can only describe as dilation. Not by velocity or gravity but by the acceptance of limit. The wall at the far end has made the distance toward it larger than it should be, each step containing more than a step should.

August. A bad week. The headaches came back, worse than before. The new MRI showed growth. His hand went to his temple before his face changed. The body always knew first. Our oncologist said "progression" and "palliative options" and "quality of remaining time." David listened, nodded, asked two precise questions about the imaging data, and on the cab ride home said: "I need to finish the Whitestone model."

Not: I'm scared. Not: Hold me. I need to finish the Whitestone model.

And I understood, and I hated it, and I also understood that hate was the wrong word for what I felt, which was something more like the ache you feel watching someone run a race you can't enter, knowing the finish line is the thing that kills them, knowing the running is the thing that makes them most alive.

He worked for nine days straight. The AI ran continuously. I brought food he sometimes ate.

The Whitestone model was a predictive framework for structural health monitoring of New York's aging bridges under climate stress, the kind of thing that, if the city ever implements it, might prevent catastrophic failures for the next century. He was building it with a brain tumor pressing against the parts of him that controlled fine motor function, so that by the end his left hand trembled on the keyboard and the AI had learned to predict the word from three shaky keystrokes, matching him the way only something that had listened for months could match.

On the ninth day he called me in. The model was on the screen, rotating slowly, a three-dimensional rendering of the bridge's structural system overlaid with probability fields for failure events under twelve different climate and load scenarios. It was beautiful. Not metaphorically. Beside the keyboard, a yellow legal pad covered in his block handwriting — load calculations, sketches of cable geometries, the analog residue of a mind that still needed to feel the pencil.

"This is what I'll leave," he said.

"David," I said. I didn't know what else to say. The model was turning on the screen and his hand was shaking and I could see both things at once.

"I know," he said. Not arrogance. Accuracy.

We sat there for a while. The model kept turning. Then, very quietly, not looking at me, he said: "I keep thinking if I go fast enough." He didn't finish. I didn't finish it for him. He looked at the screen and then at me and said, "I can't explain what I'm seeing," and I understood that this was not frustration. It was wonder.

It's October now. He sleeps more. The AI keeps running while he sleeps. He's set it to continue certain lines of inquiry, to flag things for his review, so that when he wakes, there are gifts waiting. New papers. New connections. New models half-built, waiting for the part that only he can do: the part where a human mind looks at a pattern and says *yes, that's it, that's the thing that matters.* The AI can't do that yet. So it waits for him, and he wakes, and he does the thing that only he can do, and the distance between us grows another increment.

There are good days when the gap closes. Sundays, sometimes. He'll put the screens away, all of them, a ritual, powering each one down with a deliberate press, like closing books. We'll sit on the patio and drink wine and he'll be in my time, or close to it. From the apartment above, someone practicing piano — a round, the same melody entering again and again, each voice a few beats behind the last. From the fire escape, a bird singing in sharp, irregular phrases, arriving from some direction I couldn't predict. We'll talk about the neighbor's dog, about the time we got lost in the Catskills and ended up eating dinner in a stranger's farmhouse until midnight. On those days, his eyes don't have the brightness. They have something older. Something that remembers what it was like to waste time together, to let the hours be empty and call the emptiness good.

But even on those days, I catch him. A flicker. He'll look at the fire escape garden, the tomatoes, the basil, the one stubborn morning glory vine, and I'll see something happen behind his eyes, and I'll know that some part of him is running at the other speed, even now, even here.

He asked me last week if I was okay.

"I don't know," I said.

He waited.

"I'm outside," I said. "I'm outside of whatever you're inside of, and I don't know how to describe the temperature out here."

He nodded. He was quiet for a while. A long while. I thought he might be falling asleep. Then he reached over and straightened the collar of my shirt, slowly, the way you straighten something that doesn't need straightening, and his hand stayed on my shoulder, and we sat like that until the light moved off the wall. I didn't know I touched the doorframe every time I left his room. He told me, near the end, that he'd been counting.

I think I understand now what frightens him. It isn't dying. He came back to God after twenty years away, and I think the coming back is part of what drives the work. Not because he doubts. Because he's afraid the return isn't enough on its own. That he needs to bring something with him. That the time will run out before the work is finished, and whatever he lays down will be incomplete. That's what the acceleration is. He is trying to make the offering worthy of the thing he's only just begun to believe in again. Whatever spoke to him in those three days was not general. It had his name on it.

Two clocks in the same room, ticking at different rates, each one accurate, neither one wrong. That's what marriage means now. The love is in listening to the other clock and choosing to stay.

The light has reached the far wall. It does this every afternoon at this hour, and every afternoon David watches it arrive, and every afternoon I watch him watch it. Today his eyes are half-closed. His breathing is shallow. The AI hums from the desk. He's left a model running, something about retrofit strategies for the older East River crossings, and the screen shows a bridge being reinforced by mathematics, cable by cable, decade by decade.

I take his hand. His fingers are cold. They tighten on mine, slowly, the way you hold something you know you're about to set down. There's a small tattoo on his wrist, a Japanese toad he got in his twenties, years before I knew him. Kaeru. The word means both frog and to return. He got it because he thought that was funny.

"The light," he says.

"I see it," I say.

I hold his hand. The light moves. The room holds us both.